Tim was so cu... ...around to see if I was interested in being his date instead of coming straight out and asking me.

"But what if the girl is someone who could go out with any guy in the class?" he asked, meeting my gaze.

"I'm sure she'd rather go with you than anyone else," I said softly. "You should ask her, Tim."

"Maybe you're right." He reached over and squeezed my hand, and my heart started racing with happiness.

I watched as Tim inhaled deeply. "Thanks, Annie, you really helped me make up my mind. I'll call Marcy as soon as I get home."

Bantam Sweet Dreams Romances
Ask your bookseller for the books you have missed

Ask Annie

Suzanne Rand

BANTAM BOOKS
TORONTO · NEW YORK · LONDON · SYDNEY

RL 6, IL age 11 and up

ASK ANNIE
A Bantam Book/July 1982
Reprinted 1983

Cover photo by Pat Hill.

ISBN 0-553-22518-9

Published simultaneously in the United States and Canada

---

*Bantam Books are published by Bantam Books, Inc. Its trademark,
consisting of the words "Bantam Books" and the portrayal of a rooster,
is Registered in U.S. Patent and Trademark Office and in other
countries. Marca Registrada. Bantam Books, Inc., 666 Fifth Avenue,
New York, New York 10103.*

Printed and bound in Great Britain by
Cox & Wyman Ltd, Reading

Ask Annie

Chapter One

"What do you think, Annie?" Kathy swiveled around on the bench at the dressing table to face me. "The blusher's too dark, right?"

"Not if you want to show up at school tomorrow looking like an Indian," I said, then laughed as I sat on one of her twin beds.

She sighed, then reached for a pink tissue from the box on the table and turned her back to me again while she rubbed off all the makeup.

"Face it—your skin's too light for Tropical Tan, Kathy."

"Is that a pun?" she asked, getting up

and hurling herself down on the other twin bed. "*Face* it—it's wrong for my *face*? Get it? Ha, ha. Anyhow, it's *Tahitian* Tan, and I can't believe I just blew five dollars on makeup I'll never wear."

"What made you buy a color like that?" I asked.

"Not using my brain, I guess." She smiled ruefully and ran her fingers through her carrot-colored curls. I could tell that, as always, her bad mood had passed as quickly as it had come. "I was in Marta's Beauty Shop waiting for Mom to get out from under the dryer, and I saw an ad for it in a magazine. Of course, the girl in the advertisement was skinny and dark-haired, with cheekbones that made her look like she hadn't eaten in *days*!" She heaved another sigh, living proof of why she was considered the best actress in the sophomore class.

"I just don't think it's you," I said soothingly. "You look better in peachy colors."

"What you mean is that my face is round as a cookie and white as flour, Annie Wainwright, and you know it," she corrected me, saying just what I'd been thinking. "It's not fair that Tim should get high cheekbones and long eyelashes while I end up with a face like some Irish chambermaid. Who would have thought that twins could be so different-looking?" She moaned, then pulled herself up from the bed as if she'd been lying there with the Asian flu for at least two weeks. "Let's go over to your house and do our math homework, OK? I'm dying for some of your mother's chocolate chip cookies." She looked at me critically before she switched off the light. "And you can have the blusher as a present from me. At least you've got the right coloring for it."

Later, after Kathy had gone home and I'd kissed Mom and Dad good night and was getting ready for bed, I remembered what she had said.

What exactly was the right coloring? And if mine was "right" for Tahitian Tan, did that mean it was right in general? Kathy was always laughing at her looks, calling herself "Pie Face" and "Fire-Engine Fuzz," but that was easy to do, because Kathy knew she was neat-looking in her own way. She had a kind of self-confidence I couldn't even begin to understand.

She was one of those kids who seem naturally sure of themselves without being conceited about it. In fact, that's how both O'Hara twins were. They just never seemed to worry much about what anyone else thought of them.

Actually, the entire O'Hara family was like that, all five kids and both the parents. And for that reason, ever since I was a little kid, I'd enjoyed hanging out at their house, which was right down the block from ours. Even now that Molly was married and living in New Jersey and Andy was in the navy and Teresa was away at nursing school, I liked being there. It was noisy and busy and fun.

Our house wasn't like that at all. Maybe it was because I was an only child, but we never sat around the kitchen table talking for hours like the O'Haras did when Kathy's parents came home from their jobs. When Dad walked in the door, he just sat in the living room by himself going over the insurance contracts he'd filled out that day, then read the paper. Since Mom didn't work, she was usually busy cooking, or if it was still light out, she was in the backyard working in her garden. And our kitchen table was reserved for breakfast only. We ate all other meals at the big mahogany table in the dining room.

How would Kathy feel if she had my face? I wondered as I soaped and rinsed it off over the bathroom sink. Probably just the same as she felt with her own face, I decided, answering my own question.

Kathy O'Hara wouldn't stand in front of the mirror the way I did, wondering if her olive complexion was too sallow and yellowish or if her hair was too drab a shade of brown. She'd just live with what she'd been given.

Well, so would I! I smiled at myself in the mirror, showing the teeth Dad still groaned about having gone "practically to the poorhouse" trying to get straightened. It was what I thought of as my Movie Star Smile, although I was usually too nervous to remember to dazzle anybody with it when it counted.

"Good night, gorgeous," I whispered. Then I made a face at myself, turned out the light, and went back down the hall to my room and to bed.

The next day was as bright and wonderful as a morning in late September can be. As usual, Dad had already left for work by the time I went downstairs, and Mom had started tidying up the living room, where they'd been watching TV the night before. She'd put a glass of juice on the kitchen table by my regular place, along with a bowl of cornflakes. I poured milk on them without paying much attention. My mind was already busy trying to figure out if Tim O'Hara might be leaving for school when I went to pick up Kathy. I hoped he'd be swinging himself up onto his bike the way he had one morning the week before when I'd stopped to pick her up. I looked better today, in my brand-new pair of close-fitting corduroys and a red-and-white-striped shirt, than I had then. I'd even taken pains to do what I hoped the fashion magazines meant when they talked about accentuating your cheekbones, carefully blending Tahitian Tan all the way up to my temples.

I don't know what it was about Tim O'Hara, but I'd had a crush on him for almost as long as I could remember, and instead of dying down, it kept growing stronger. This year was the worst ever. Tim and Kathy had spent the last part of the summer traveling with their parents through Canada in a rented camper and when they came back, Tim seemed taller and better-looking than I could have imagined.

But he didn't seem to notice me any more than he had when we were all in third grade together and I was layered with what my mother politely called "baby fat." My baby fat had hung on to become teenage fat, though. Oh, I was never a blimp or anything, but up until this past summer I'd have given a million dollars to wring the neck of whatever smart-aleck salesperson or designer thought up the term "Chubbette." Nothing can be worse than having your mother dragging you around a shop and asking salespeople, "Can you tell us where the Chubbette dresses are?"

Anyhow, when we started ninth grade and went to Castle Heights High instead of the familiar old red brick junior high school, I just couldn't handle being pleasantly plump anymore. I'd look around at all the skinny junior and senior girls and feel like a relative of the Goodyear blimp. No boy would ever notice me as long as I was five feet, four inches tall and tipped the scales at 140—why should he? That's why I made up my mind to go on a diet.

Of course, making up your mind to go on a diet and doing it are two different things, and I was too busy feeling out of place to find the time to stop shoving food in my mouth. But when summer came, it was a different story.

As soon as school was out, I enrolled at the local swim club. I forced myself to bike or walk the mile to and from the pool every day, and I forced myself to swim five, then ten, and then twenty laps.

I even got up my nerve to tell Mom I was trying to lose weight and to ask her not to make desserts for me anymore. I was sure she'd make some remark about how I was just a little girl and not overweight at all, so you can imagine how surprised I was when she said, "Of course, darling. I didn't realize you were trying to cut down." She even made a point of patting her own perfectly flat stomach and saying, "I guess we could all stand to lose a pound or two. From now on, it's going to be diet meals all the way!"

See, that's the thing about my mother, and my father, too, really. They're not outgoing and openly affectionate and casual like the O'Haras, but they mean well. I think they're both shy. Maybe that's why I turned out shy. Who knows?

To get back to the point of this whole

story, by the time Kathy and Tim returned from Canada at the end of August, I was a slim and trim 115 pounds. When Kathy came over to my house to tell me they were home again, she gasped as I opened the door. "Annie Wainwright, you look fantastic! Now we can borrow each other's clothes!" That's Kathy, always practical.

Well, of course I was dying for Tim to see the new me. But do you know what he said when he did? He was out mowing the lawn when I walked past the O'Hara place on my way to the grocery store, and he waved and called, "Hey, Annie, how's it going? Do anything exciting this summer?"

"Not really," I said, waiting for his eyes to widen in surprise at the change in me. "Just a lot of swimming over at the pool."

"I guess Kathy already told you about our trip," he went on as if I were the same butterball as before. "Boy, did we have a terrific time!"

"Mmm," I murmured, not having the faintest idea what to say next. "That's great." I waited just long enough to see if he was suddenly going to clutch his heart and proclaim that I was beautiful. He didn't, so I just sort of muttered, "Well, see you around," then slunk off.

I mean, he hardly even noticed me!

Now, as I walked along the street in the direction of Kathy's house, I wondered if Tim O'Hara had ever really noticed me in all those years we'd been neighbors. I had a feeling the answer was no, and it made me feel as tongue-tied and out of it as when I used to think of myself as an Oven-Stuffed roaster.

As I got closer to the O'Haras' white frame house, I could see Tim kneeling by the garage and hear the swoosh of his bicycle pump as he concentrated on putting more air in his tires. I walked a little faster, trying to get to the driveway before he took off.

Then I slowed down again. I liked watching Tim without his knowing it. He had wonderful dark, curly hair, and a long, lean body. When we were all little, Tim and Kathy were almost the same size. Then, the summer we were thirteen, he shot up. Now Tim was a good six feet tall. Kathy was still a shrimp, just a little over five feet tall, and round all over without being fat.

And she'd been right about their cheek-bones. From where I was, I could see the angles of his face. With his summer tan, he looked almost like a handsome Indian brave. Only Kathy and Tim's snub noses, both dusted with freckles, and their sparkling green eyes were proof that they were twins.

My eyes must have been practically boring holes in Tim's head, because just as I got to the foot of the driveway, he looked up. You'd have thought maybe he'd wait and talk to me, but no such luck. Even as I was running up to the house, he cuffed his jeans so they wouldn't get caught, swung one leg over the bike, and coasted down the gentle slope of the driveway.

"Hi, Tim!" I called brightly when he was several feet from where I was standing.

"Hey, Annie! Great day, isn't it?" His face was open and friendly, and I knew I should have been able to answer him just as casually, but I couldn't. He wasn't just Tim O'Hara, Kathy's brother. He was a boy, *the* boy. My tongue felt as if it were made of lead. I couldn't make it move to say the things I wanted to say. I tried nodding and smiling, but I knew my smile was tight and prim-looking, as if I were afraid my teeth would fall out. My Movie Star Smile deserted me completely.

Tim stopped next to me, lowering one foot from the pedal and scuffing to a stop. He bounced gently up and down on the seat. "Darn back tire's got a slow leak, I think," he said, as much to himself as to me. "I pumped it full of air, and it still feels low."

"I saw you working on it," I said, knowing it was a dumb thing to say but wanting to keep him there just a minute longer. I narrowed my eyes and looked at the tire as if I were an expert on bikes. "It looks OK, though."

"I guess I'll make it as far as school." He grinned, and I smiled back. Castle Heights High was only about eight blocks from our street.

I heard the screen door bang shut as Kathy bounded out, and I desperately tried to think of something else to say before she reached us. "Maybe you should take it to the garage and have it checked."

"Yeah, one of these days." He smiled and shrugged, then giving a little wave of his hand, he swung himself back onto the seat and pedaled off.

"Sorry it took me so long!" Kathy was frantically stuffing papers and books into her knapsack as she rushed up to me. "I couldn't remember where I'd put my math papers when I got home last night. Someday I really am going to get organized," she vowed, even though she knew as well as I did that she'd never do it. Being scatterbrained was part of Kathy's personality, and sometimes I thought she actually worked at it because her craziness kept kids from noticing that she was a straight-A student.

She talked on and on as we walked to school. "So now Mom says," she wailed, "that if I don't get my closet straightened out by tomorrow afternoon, I can't go to the movies Saturday night. And I know it's going to take me *days* to get it done!"

I nodded, even though I wasn't really listening to what she was saying. I was too busy listening to the echo of my own voice reverberating in my head. *Maybe you should take it to the garage and have it checked.* How could I have said such a dumb thing to Tim after waiting all this time to talk to him? I'd been so boring it probably didn't even matter that I was thin.

As soon as we got to school, I stowed my things in my locker and then hurried up to the second floor. I reached the checkout desk of the big, musty-smelling library just as the first homeroom bell started clanging.

Mrs. DeWitt, the gray-haired librarian everybody called "The Prune" behind her back because she was so dry and wrinkled and sour, gave me a look of stern approval over the top of her harlequin glasses as she stamped the take-out slip glued to the inside cover of *A Trip Through the Canadian Wilderness.*

"Here you are, Miss Wainwright," she said, pushing the book back across the linoleum counter to me. Mrs. DeWitt never called anyone by his or her first name. She probably even called her husband Mr. DeWitt. "It's nice to see that some students are still so interested in broadening their minds that they come to the library before homeroom." Her face grew longer before my eyes, and she closed her eyes as if her head hurt. "In my day, young people weren't expected to ignore good books. But that was before television, of course."

"Thank you, Mrs. DeWitt," I said hastily. I snatched up the heavy book and dashed off to homeroom. I didn't feel like listening to another one of Mrs. DeWitt's lectures about the evils of TV. Besides, I couldn't help feeling guilty, as if she'd just caught me in a great big lie. I mean, here she thought I was some kind of scholar when my only interest in Canada was how I could use the subject to get a date with my best friend's brother!

Chapter Two

I got my chance to show off my knowledge of Canada to Tim the very next day.

His bike wasn't at the O'Haras' when I stopped by for Kathy on the way to school, and I figured he'd already left. It was a Friday, so I was a little down because of missing him, especially since I'd stayed up half the night reading about camping out in the wilds of Canada, something that sounded about as much fun as standing in front of a firing squad.

Tim was in only one of my classes. Even though we were both in the tenth grade, Castle Heights was a big school, the biggest of all in the Philadelphia suburbs, so it wasn't odd that our only shared class was fifth-period American history. And since Mr. Petrowski, the gnarled old goat who taught us, was a big believer in the old alphabetical seating order, it meant Tim sat in the middle of the third row while I was stuck in the next-to-last seat in the entire classroom, right in front of Albert Zimmer.

As Kathy and I were walking to school, I was fretting over the prospect of having to review my Canadian wilderness book Sunday night. Then Kathy's voice cut into my thoughts. We were just about a block from the big two-story grey granite building jokingly called Castle Heights County Jail, when she exclaimed in the breathy, excited voice she saved for all big news, "I forgot to tell you, Annie! I can't believe it!"

"Can't believe what?" I knew Kathy was dying to tell me whatever it was, but I also knew her well enough to realize she loved building up the suspense and making the most of her news, so I didn't ask for specifics right away.

"Don't you know what day this is?" she asked, acting secretive.

I shrugged. "Friday. It comes once a week."

"No, not just Friday, stupid!" she said teasingly.

I studied her, trying to puzzle it out. She was wearing a really nice high-necked navy knit dress and red leather ballet slippers, which she had once called her "actressy" outfit, so I guessed it had something to do with the drama department, but I decided to torment her a little.

"That's right, I forgot!" I said. "It's the day you've got to straighten up your closet if you don't want to be grounded tomorrow night."

She rolled her eyes melodramatically. "Don't be so dense, Annie! Besides, I got that done last night."

"I give up, then," I said nonchalantly as we walked through the big oak doors of the school's main entrance, weaving our way through little groups of kids standing around talking and waiting until the first bell.

"It's sophomore class play auditions today!" She grabbed my arm, and I could feel the excitement racing through her. "This year they're doing *Our Town*. Don't you think I'd be a perfect Emily?"

I couldn't help but laugh. "I think Emily was a little more on the modest side," I reminded her. Then seeing her face fall, I added quickly, "But other than that, yes, I think you'd be great."

"Oh, I'm dying to get the part." She moaned, but her face looked normal again, and she seemed happy enough. That's the thing with Kathy. The slightest thing can make her depressed, but a second later she's forgotten about it. I guess that's what's called an artistic temperament. I'm more the plodding type, which suits someone who wants to be a reporter. I don't get mad or glad or anything very quickly, but once I get settled into any mood, it takes an earthquake to shake me out of it.

The bell rang for homeroom. "I've got to run for it," I said quickly. Kathy's homeroom was right by the ground-floor auditorium, but mine was way down at the end of one of the creaking second-floor corridors, the old part of the building, which had been Castle Heights High in its entirety back in the fifties.

"Well, I just wanted to let you know I can't walk home with you tonight 'cause of auditions," Kathy called after me. "And I've got to practice my scenes during lunch."

"OK," I yelled back over my shoulder. "Call me at home tonight and let me know how it went. And good luck!"

I didn't mind that Kathy had other things to do. It wasn't as if we were joined at the waist or anything. Oh, we'd been inseparable through eighth grade, but since we'd started at the senior high, both of us had made other close friends and found our own interests. Kathy had her plays and the drama society, and I had my work on the *Turret*, the school paper. I was really proud to be connected with the paper, even though as a sophomore I got most of the lowly jobs, like delivering the copies to homerooms every other week and proofreading. But once in a while, Deanna Hackett, the editor and a senior, or Mr. Jensen, the faculty adviser, gave me a small assignment. When that happened, I labored over the piece as if I were eligible for the Pulitzer Prize.

So today I had lunch with Carole Deutsch, and later I was perfectly happy to walk home from school by myself. The next night Kathy and I were planning to go to the new Woody Allen movie, so I didn't miss her company too much.

I was about a block and a half from school

when I spied Tim's back a few hundred feet ahead of me. And he was walking by himself!

I took hasty, silent steps so I could catch up to him without his knowing. I figured Tim was polite enough to walk with me whether he wanted to or not.

Since I was concentrating so hard on sneaking up behind him, he didn't hear me, even when I was about ten feet in back of him. But I didn't have the nerve to spring myself on him, so I forced out a tiny cough and started scuffing my feet on the sidewalk.

He turned his head and caught sight of me out of the corner of his eye. "Hi, Annie. What're you doing walking home alone?" Before I could answer, he answered his own question. "Oh, that's right. Kathy's auditioning for the play, isn't she?"

"Yes." I giggled, feeling my cheeks growing hot now that he was actually right next to me, keeping in step with my stride, which I slowed down since I wanted to drag out this walk as long as I could. "She says she'll make the *perfect* Emily for *Our Town*," I added, stressing the words as blatantly as Kathy always did.

He smiled crookedly, and my heart lurched inside my chest, feeling as if it were banging

21

against my ribs. "That kid'll end up on Broadway yet," he said, sounding like a proud father even though he was only four minutes older. "She was really upset about having to go to Canada during the summer and not being able to help out at the little theater."

It sounded like the perfect opening, and I grabbed it. "I'd give anything to go to Canada," I lied. "I've heard the sunsets in Banff are unbelievable. I'd just love to sit and watch the sun setting behind the"—I fumbled for an instant, trying to remember what I'd read in the book—"fir trees, to see the reflection all red and gold in the lake!"

"Yeah, I'd like to see that part of the country someday, too," he said eagerly. "We didn't get that far west. We stayed pretty close to the big cities. I really dug Montreal. It was great."

My knowing smile died on my lips. I'd been so pleased with myself for thinking up my plan to find something to talk to Tim about that I hadn't even bothered trying to remember where Kathy had said they'd been. My book had nothing at all in it about the big cities! "You mean you didn't go to the wilderness?" I asked.

I guess I sounded sort of upset, because

Tim gave me a strange look. "Nope. But I'd like to go there sometime," he added, as if he wanted to calm me down.

I felt like a fool. We walked along without saying a word while I tried to think of something else to say that wouldn't sound totally retarded. Luckily, Tim started to speak first.

"I had to leave my bike at school," he said, explaining why he was walking. "The tire's dead, and I won't be able to buy a new one until I get my paycheck from Armor's on Monday."

"Oh, are you still working there?" I asked. Armor's was the grocery store in our neighborhood, and Tim had worked there after school for a year now.

"Just Saturday afternoons and Thursday nights. I want the extra time after school so I can go out for the basketball team. I'm eligible for varsity this year."

"That's great!" I exclaimed. Hadn't I read somewhere you were always supposed to be enthusiastic when someone talked about his or her plans and dreams?

"Yeah." He didn't sound too happy. "At least, it *would* be great if my mother would just relax about it. Team tryouts start next month, and already she's saying it might be better if I don't go out for it."

"How come?"

He shrugged. "My grades slipped last year when I was on the junior varsity team. I keep trying to convince Mom that that won't happen this year since I won't be working so hard at Armor's, but she still hasn't said OK." He sighed, almost as theatrically as Kathy usually did. "I can't tell you how bummed out I'll be if she says no."

It was time to put my reporter's insight to use, I thought, turning Tim's problem around in my mind. I was more interested in keeping the talk flowing than in getting him on the basketball team, but I wasn't completely selfish. He looked so miserable just thinking about not being able to play ball that I was determined to help him.

"Maybe you should try to make a deal with her," I suggested brightly, as if I handed out advice to great-looking boys every day of my life.

Well, at least I'd gotten his interest. "What do you mean?" he asked, stopping right there in the middle of the sidewalk and staring at me. "What kind of a deal?"

"Just a deal," I said calmly. I started walking again so Tim wouldn't notice I felt anything but calm. I mean, the nerve of me, giving Tim O'Hara my worldly wisdom on how to handle his mother!

"Just ask her to give you a two-month trial," I went on, fighting to keep my voice light and casual. "If your grades aren't up in two months, you agree to quit the team without another word. If they're good, she agrees not to hassle you about basketball anymore."

He walked along by my side without saying anything, and I was almost scared to look over at him, afraid I'd see his face all screwed up in disgust as he thought to himself how stupid I was. But when I finally did glance at his face I was rewarded by the sight of Tim nodding his head and smiling slightly.

"Not a bad idea!" he finally said. "Not bad at all!"

We'd reached the sidewalk in front of his house then, and as we stopped, Tim tilted his head a little, and his gorgeous green eyes looked straight into mine. It was as if he were seeing me as a real person for the first time ever. Finally. Do you know how long I'd been dying for that to happen?

"Hey, thanks a lot, kid." It was all I could do not to burst with happiness when he reached over and gave one of my shoulders a little pat. "I'll let you know how everything turns out."

He started to walk away, then turned back. "By the way, have I told you how great you look? Really terrific lately." His cheeks reddened a little, and then he raised his hand in a mock salute. "Thanks for the help."

I floated the rest of the way home, a good two feet off the ground, I think. Even the fact that Tim had called me "kid" didn't take the glow off his words. I was as ecstatic and light-headed as if he'd called me "darling." Because for the first time since I'd known him, I'd gotten up enough nerve to talk to Tim as though I were mature and not the slightest bit unsure about what to say to a boy. And it had worked. He'd finally taken a good long look at the new Annie Wainwright!

Chapter Three

I hadn't always been afraid of boys. Back in the third and fourth grades, I was even a bit of a tomboy. Kathy was, too, and that's how we got to be such good friends. The two of us were always pestering Tim and his friends to let us play baseball, basketball, or football with them. Even when we got to sixth grade, we were much more likely to be bugging Andy O'Hara to take us fishing with him out by the old pond on Route 12 than to be tagging around after Molly and Teresa, whose interest in makeup, record collections, and boys we thought just plain idiotic.

When I turned twelve, Mom and Dad gave

me a new watch, the bright blue ski parka I wanted, and fifty dollars to do with as I pleased. Mom also gave me a big talk about puberty.

Mostly she told me things I already knew, about how I'd be getting my period soon and how my body would be changing. She kept referring to it as "becoming a young woman," her small, dark face all screwed up the way it gets when she's trying to be serious.

I could tell Mom wasn't comfortable talking to me about it by the way she kept licking her lips every time she stopped for breath. It was as if she worried that someone might hear her and think she was explaining it all wrong.

Finally she made me nervous, the way she kept saying, "Now, do you understand, Annie?" and then rattling on before I had a chance to answer. Maybe she was scared I was going to ask her something she wouldn't want to answer. Anyway, when I could get a word in, I said, "It's OK, Mom. Mrs. Bendix at school already told us all this stuff. Can I go do my homework now?"'

She let me go then, and I could tell she was as happy to have the talk over with as I was. The only problem was, neither Mom nor

Mrs. Bendix ever got around to explaining why all of a sudden boys turned into the enemy.

Oh, I don't mean I saw them as horrible torturers or anything like that. It was just that the older I got, the more I realized how *different* they were. They knew it, too, because eventually Tim and his friends would go out of their way to ditch us every time they saw us. Andy still let us trail around after him, but I could tell he thought of us as just a couple of kids and not his equals, so it wasn't the same.

By the time I started junior high school, I could barely say two words to a boy, unless he was somebody like Marshall Todman, who didn't seem to realize girls existed and probably never would. When I was around cute guys like Tim or Billy Ray, my lips went as numb as if the dentist had just shot me up with Novocain—and my brain followed.

By ninth grade I was blaming it all on my weight. I guess as long as I could tell myself I was so fat no boy would ask me out, I could overlook the fact that I blushed and stuttered around all of them. But I couldn't hide one thing from myself—and that was how badly I wanted a boyfriend.

I knew other girls went out on dates, to games and school dances and things like that. Kathy had at least ten dates in the ninth grade, and she'd even told me that when she'd gone to a night game with Kevin Thomas, who was a year ahead of us in school, they'd spent most of halftime necking out by the parking lot. "He's such a good kisser, Annie!" she said, simpering in a way that made me want to slug her. "I wish more boys knew how to kiss right, don't you?"

I nodded noncommittally and switched the subject back to the basketball scores. I didn't want even Kathy to know I'd never kissed anybody.

By now some of the girls I hung around with even had steady boyfriends. Sandy Collins wore Doug Ruffner's signet ring on a delicate gold chain around her neck and spent all her free time dangling from his arm like a live ID bracelet or snuggling up to him in the corridors as if the temperature in the school building had dropped below zero. The only reason she still sat with us in the cafeteria was because the school officials had cruelly overlooked the path of true love and given Doug and her different lunch periods.

So here I was, finally thin and decent-looking, still cringing at the embarrassing words that would come from between my stiff lips whenever I tried to talk to a guy. But now I'd talked to not just any guy, but to Tim O'Hara, and with such coolness, he probably thought I walked home with tall, adorable basketball players all the time.

I didn't let myself think about it too much the next few days, though. I mean, I did have a crush on Tim, and I was as excited about having a real conversation with him as if he had been the president of the United States, but I knew better than to let myself get carried away. It might never happen again, so I was determined to keep it in proper perspective. If nothing else, I was making headway in fighting my shyness.

And then, without warning, just a week later, something happened that brought Tim into the very center of my life. I'd already learned, from pumping Kathy as offhandedly as possible, that Mrs. O'Hara had agreed to Tim's "deal" about playing basketball. This, of course, caused me to feel pleased with myself.

We were enjoying a bright, crisp October week, full of the kind of days that make you feel everything's right with the whole world.

Even my mother and father seemed more cheerful than usual. Dad had gotten a raise and been promoted to sales manager at his insurance firm, and he acted as if a great weight had been lifted. He even came home with a bottle of champagne one night and insisted Mom let me have a glass with them after dinner. It occurred to me that maybe Mom and Dad had seemed vague and disinterested lately because their minds had been on the possibility of this promotion. Then when Mom toasted Dad with her champagne, in the good crystal glasses she brought out only for special occasions, and said, "Here's to finally paying off the station wagon!" I knew I was right and that money had been worrying both of them recently.

Kathy was full of energy that week, too, even though another girl had gotten the role of Emily in *Our Town*. Kathy had gotten a supporting part, which was more than made up for by the fact that she'd be playing opposite Kurt Mauer. "Can't you just see our names on a marquee one day, Annie?" She sighed. "Kathy and Kurt . . . Kurt and Kathy. . . . Ooo, he's like a Greek god with that blond hair and those big shoulders!" It wasn't hard to guess she was in love.

I wasn't jealous, though—I was too busy carrying out a plan I had devised. I knew I had to work on getting over my shyness, so I decided that every time I would pass a boy I knew in the halls, I would give him a big hello, and whenever I got the chance, I'd force myself to make small talk. It wasn't easy at first, but the more I managed to do it, the less I saw boys as some alien race and the easier it got.

And then one day as I was leaving the cafeteria, Tim called me over to where he was sitting with his friends. "Hey, Annie! Come here for a sec!"

I recognized the voice even before I turned around. Tim was sitting with two other guys I knew, Kenny Farrell and Barry Goldstein. I could feel their eyes on me as I moved toward them, and I concentrated hard on walking with a bounce in my step so nobody could guess how shaky and jellyish my knees felt at that moment.

Eat your hearts out, girls, I thought brazenly as I passed the table where Dee Caldwell and Marcy Cummings were sitting, their lunch trays spread in front of them like newspapers they'd suddenly lost interest in reading. I felt a little thrill of triumph when I saw the expression of disbelief on Marcy's face. Her lips were pursed as if she'd just bitten into a sour pickle, and I could tell she was trying to pretend she hadn't noticed me. I almost giggled when I heard her complain to Dee as I passed, "Tim O'Hara's so loud! He always has to be the center of attention!"

What Marcy was really doing was describing herself. Tim was popular, but he was no egomaniac. Marcy, on the other hand, could have won an Oscar for demanding attention. Even when we were kids, Mrs. Cummings had always treated her like a china doll, dressing her up in ruffled pinafores just to go to Castle Heights Grammar School and get all muddy playing kick-it-and-run. Not that Marcy was ever much of a kicker. Even then, she'd just tap the ball with her patent-leather Mary Janes in a ladylike manner, as if she were above it all.

When she'd discovered boys, Marcy had gotten even more unbearable. She was the class flirt, always batting her baby blues and tossing her straight corn-colored hair around like a matador waving down a bull. I knew she'd give anything for a chance at Tim O'Hara—or any other guy in the school, for that matter. And she'd always treated me as if I didn't exist, except for one day in grammar school when I'd crossed the asphalt of the playground to see if anybody in the little group around her wanted to play jacks with me. "Go away, fatty," she'd spat at me. "Nobody here wants to play with you."

So you can see why I was so pleased at making her jealous—and I could tell from the nasty note in her voice that she certainly was jealous!

Suddenly I felt powerful, and I liked the way it felt. By the time I walked up to where Tim sat with the other guys, I had a big grin on my face.

"Hi, Tim," I said easily. "What's up?"

Now that he'd gotten me over there, he looked as if he didn't quite know what to say. "Um—it's about Kenny here. He's having a problem with his father, and I was telling him how your advice about my mother helped me."

"Yeah, so I decided to put my life in your hands." Kenny winked, and Barry laughed and poked him in the ribs with his elbow.

I didn't say anything at first. I just stood there, looking from one of them to the other, trying to figure out if they were making fun of me.

Finally Tim came to my rescue. I guess

he was peeved that the guys were acting like it was a big joke. "Look, Kenny, do you want to sit there laughing like an idiot, or are you going to tell Annie what's wrong?" he asked, exasperated.

Kenny grew serious. "OK," he said, his smile disappearing. "The old man says he doesn't see why he should let me use the car on Saturday nights." He shot a disgusted look at no one in particular, and I could tell he was really upset. "I know it's not that he doesn't trust me. He's just being difficult."

"I told Kenny if anybody could give good advice it was you, Annie," Tim said, his eyes looking into mine in a solemn way that made me feel like laughing and crying at the same time.

I could barely think, much less talk, because my heart was someplace in the vicinity of my throat. Thank goodness Barry broke the tension. " 'Dear Annie,' " he said in a deep, announcer-type voice, reading from an imaginary newspaper he held in front of him. " 'Please help me! I've got this terrible problem. . . .' "

I smiled weakly. Then Kenny said kiddingly, "Boy, I'll say, Goldstein! Have you ever got problems!"

We all laughed, and it felt as if a fog of nerve gas hanging over the table had just been blown away.

"So what do you say, Annie?" Tim asked. "Got any ideas for Kenny?" He rolled his eyes toward Barry. "We know you haven't got time even to *begin* working on Barry's problems."

I giggled, but in relief instead of nervousness this time. They were treating me just like one of the guys, friendly and casual, and I didn't feel the slightest bit intimidated by them anymore.

"Why not tell your dad you'll earn the use of the car?" I suggested, keeping my tone mature and, I hoped, wise. "Maybe he'll change his mind if you tell him that you'll take care of gassing it up every week and checking the oil and stuff like that."

"Yeah, Kenny," Barry said, in his best Godfather imitation. "Make him an offer he can't refuse."

They were all laughing but not, I realized, at me, so I joined in, too. "It may not be the greatest idea," I said, shrugging, "but it's the best I've got."

"Not bad," Tim said slowly, nodding his head as if he were Kenny's agent or something. "What do you think, Farrell?"

"It's worth a shot," Kenny said, sounding mildly encouraged. "At this point I'll try anything."

"Oh, yeah? Are you serious?" Barry asked. "Really? You'd try *anything*? You'd try being rude to your grandmother? Tangling with a wolverine? ..." The boys were starting to sound vaguely hysterical, so I waited until there was a pause in their conversation, if you could call it that, before I stood up. "I've got to go," I said lightly, wanting to leave before they began trying to figure how to get rid of me. "Hope I helped you, Kenny."

"Yeah, thanks a lot, Annie," he said distractedly, already too involved with the guys to be concerned about what we'd just discussed.

So I stood there feeling awkward, not really knowing what to say next or how to make a graceful getaway, until Tim rescued me again. "You're the greatest, Annie," he said, beaming at me with a grin that put my Movie Star Smile to shame. "You got me on the basketball team—and I'll be grateful to you forever for that."

"Oh, it was nothing, Tim," I said sincerely. "Honest."

"Oh, yes, it was *something*, Annie," he insisted, "and you're really something, too!"

After that, it was easy just to float away! I seemed to be floating a lot lately.

Chapter Four

From that day on, my life was changed. More and more boys went out of their way to talk to me—especially if something was bothering them.

It was all just coincidence, really. After I helped Kenny, Barry Goldstein asked for suggestions on how to escape taking his math exam (I couldn't give him a single decent idea on *that* useless question), and then Doug Ruffner, a friend of Kenny's, approached me in the hall.

Doug and his girlfriend Sandy had apparently had a big fight over whether her skirt was too tight and whether she could wear whatever she pleased when she was going steady. Doug came to me for hints on how to handle her. Can you imagine? *I*, who had never been on anything even resembling a date!

Not that I admitted that lack to Doug. I just tried to put myself in Sandy's place and feel what she'd feel. Finally I said, "How about complimenting her whenever she wears something you *do* like and just ignoring the times she wears something you hate? After all, she dresses to please herself as well."

All this advice-giving soon made me the center of attention whenever a gang of guys was around. Well, not always, of course, but often enough so that I enjoyed it. It was as if I'd found a real identity for myself, you know? As long as I was talking to the guys about whatever was bothering them, I didn't feel so tongue-tied and out of control. I was mostly listening anyway, and when I *did* talk, I could be sure it was a subject they were interested in—themselves! They never had to listen to anything about me.

I could tell that some of the other girls didn't like what was happening, though. Oh, no one said anything at first, but I'd catch them rolling their eyes at each other or exchanging knowing looks whenever some guy came up to talk to me before class or in the lunchroom. But I was too happy with my new role to care. I was even thinking of offering to write an advice column for the school paper.

Sometimes, though, when I was all alone, I did feel a little like a fraud. You know what I mean? Here I was giving advice to these guys about all sorts of things I really knew nothing about. The freakiest thing was that most of the time my guidance paid off.

The other thing that bothered me was that I didn't seem to be much closer to having any sort of social life than I'd been when I was doing my silent routine with the opposite sex. But I kept telling myself that it was just a matter of time. At least guys were noticing me now and seeing me as a real person.

The best—and the worst—part was that Tim O'Hara was relying on me more and more for my ideas on things he was mixed-up about. Since Kathy was busy most days after school with rehearsals for the play, I usually walked home alone. But half the time, I'd find Tim catching up with me before I got too far from school. And, believe me, that fifty percent made everything else worthwhile, even listening to the moaning and groaning of boys who bored me and whose problems I considered easy to deal with.

I just *knew* that soon Tim would ask me for a date. Hadn't he even confessed once that he'd never found a girl as easy to talk to as I was?

Plus, he had let me know that he'd noticed my new, improved figure. "Kathy's been grumbling about putting on weight lately," he told me one afternoon when we were scuffling along through the red and gold leaves carpeting the sidewalk. "Maybe you should talk to her, Annie. After all, if you managed to do it, she should be able to." He hunched up his shoulders inside his wool basketball jacket then, as if he were afraid he'd said the wrong thing. "Oh, not that you were ever fat or anything," he said quickly. "But you sure did get, uh, *svelte* over the summer."

I felt a warm glow of pleasure spread through me that not even the late October winds could drive away. *Svelte*. I only wished I weren't wearing my polo coat, which covered up all my freshly chiseled curves.

"Thanks, Tim," I said. "For noticing, I

mean. I'll try to give Kathy all the best diet hints as soon as I get the chance."

But I didn't really get a chance, because the next time I saw Kathy, which was the following morning, we got into a terrible argument.

Kathy didn't say much during the first two blocks after I picked her up, and I could tell something was on her mind. But neither of us ever tried to push the other into sharing secrets until she was ready, so I just let it go, first talking about nothing in particular, then finally being as quiet as she was. Who wanted to talk if your listener didn't even nod or mumble "uh-huh" every so often?

When she finally broke the silence, her words came as a complete shock. "You know, Annie," she said, taking a deep breath and talking in a high, faltering voice that meant she was having trouble saying what was on her mind, "I really think you're acting foolish."

Immediately I put up my barriers. The slightest bit of criticism causes me to do this. "Oh?" I said, very vague and nonchalant, as if she hadn't just dropped an H-bomb on me.

Kathy had known me long enough to recognize my signals. "Now, don't close your ears and tune me out until I'm finished, Annie," she hurried on, almost pleading. "Maybe I shouldn't say this, but I'm worried because some of the girls have said things about you in front of me." She took a deep breath. "They just don't understand why you're not on their side, Annie, why you've suddenly started becoming some kind of den mother to all the guys."

"I'm hardly their den mother," I said lightly, hoping she'd drop the whole thing. "I'm too young for that."

But my comment only fired her up. "You know what I mean," she said, sounding peeved. "All of a sudden you've become the Miss Lonelyhearts of Castle Heights High. I don't think there's a girl in the entire sophomore class who doesn't know the boys go running to *you* whenever they've got a problem. And what I can't figure out is why you'd ever want to be another Ann Landers in the first place."

Now it was my turn to be annoyed. "Really, Kathy, just because I've given advice to a boy once or twice doesn't mean I'm the enemy. And it doesn't mean I want to be Ann Landers, either," I added, forgetting that I'd actually been thinking of doing a column for the paper. "And what's the big deal anyway? So what if the guys like me and want to talk over problems?"

"It's not that it's a big deal. It's just that some of the girls are getting sick of their boyfriends running to you every time a teacher yells at them or they're not allowed out by their parents. Some of the girls," she said pointedly, "think it's none of your business."

"And what do you think, Kathy?" My voice came out sounding all hard and dead, not like me at all. I could hear the blood pounding in my temples. It had never occurred to me that anyone would resent my friendships, and it certainly hadn't entered my mind that Kathy would be bothered by it.

She shrugged, and when she started talking again, her voice was unnaturally cheery, as if she were trying to balance out the weight of what she was saying. "I think you're wasting your time. *And* being used. Take Tim, for instance," she added, and my heart almost stopped.

"What about him?" I challenged her.

"Well, if you weren't there to tell him what to do all the time, he'd figure it out soon enough on his own. Not to mention the fact that my darling twin is so pigheaded he never really listens to *any* advice. He probably just likes to hear the sound of his own voice when he's talking to you, and he's using you as some kind of confessional booth."

I started walking again, slowly and with my back straight and my shoulders feeling tight and strained. "You know, Kathy," I said in a terribly unconcerned voice, "if you weren't talking about your own brother, I'd think you were jealous."

"Jealous?" She sounded genuinely surprised. "Don't be silly, Annie! Of course I'm not jealous. For one thing, I think what you're doing is all wrong. I mean, I can't imagine wanting to be one of the boys. All that'll get you is a lot of hassles. It sure won't get you a date for the Soph Hop."

Something inside me snapped at that, and the coolness I'd put on like a costume went with it. "If you know so much about how to treat boys, Kathy O'Hara," I practically snarled, "how come all you do is stare at Kurt Mauer from across the room? How come he's never asked you out? Answer that!"

We had reached the front steps of the

school by that time, and she turned away to dart up the stairs and through the door. But not before I'd seen her face crumple as if I'd hit her; not before I'd seen the tears well up in her eyes.

"Wait, Kathy—" I began apologetically, reaching out to stop her, knowing I'd said something thoughtlessly cruel.

She whirled around. "Forget it, Annie," she said coldly, in control of herself again. "Forget I said anything to you. I was just trying to help. But obviously you can only give advice, not take it. I hope you know what you're doing." Shaking her head, she walked away.

I absolutely *stalked* through the halls and up to my homeroom. I'd never known it was really possible to shake with indignation, but now I was shaking from head to toe. Of all the nerve, I thought furiously. What made Kathy O'Hara think she could tell me how to live my life?

By first period, though, I'd calmed down, and my thoughts started to travel in a different direction. I had to admit that Kathy had been very hesitant about bringing up the subject, as if she'd known it would rub me the wrong way but felt she had to say something.

She'd also done nothing worse than what I was doing lately. The only difference was, I hadn't asked for her opinion. But now that I'd gotten it, I was stuck with it, and I couldn't keep her words from running through my head. But I still thought she was wrong.

I didn't want our friendship to get awkward and stiff the way friendships do when people quarrel and don't try to straighten things out. I didn't see Kathy at lunch when we might have had a chance to talk, so I waited in front of the auditorium after school, knowing she'd have to show up sooner or later for rehearsal.

Kids in the cast were filtering into the auditorium, and the ones I knew said hello to me as they went in. At first I worried that Kathy wasn't going to come for some reason. Then I saw her walking down the hall. She was smiling up at Kurt Mauer, laughing at something he'd said, and she didn't see me watching them.

She looked like a different person. Instead of her usual ear-to-ear grin, Kathy was smiling gently. When she laughed, it was soft and whispery. And for once, Kathy seemed content to let somebody else do the talking. She wasn't saying much at all, and when she did open her mouth, I could tell it was just to let out a "great" or "interesting" or something boring like that.

And you know what? Kurt Mauer was eating it up. His blue eyes were lit up and animated. And although he had a reputation for being quiet, he appeared to be talking nonstop.

As they got closer to the door where I was waiting, Kathy spotted me, and her expression changed from delight to a sort of nervous exasperation.

"Hi, Kathy," I said carefully. "Can I talk to you for just a sec before rehearsal?"

She hesitated, biting her lip, and I was sure she wanted to tell me to get lost so she could go in with Kurt. But Kathy wasn't like that, and I didn't doubt that our snapping at each other earlier had bothered her as much as me.

Still, she wasn't going to give me the pleasure of knowing that if she could help it. Her eyes widened. "Talk to *me*, Annie?" she said in mock surprise, as if there were five or six other Kathys standing there whom I might have meant. She caught Kurt's quizzical eye and shrugged. "I'll see you in a minute or two, Kurt."

"Sure, Kath. I'll save you a seat." He nodded to me as he swung through the door to the auditorium.

Kathy slouched against the wall next to the glass showcase that held Castle Heights High School's sports and scholarship trophies. "What's up, Annie?"

"I just wanted to say I'm sorry about this morning. I know you weren't trying to be mean or anything. I just think you're wrong," I added. I don't know why, but I felt I had to qualify my apology, to let her know I was only saying I was sorry because I thought she was too good a friend to lose, not because she had a point.

But it seemed as if Kathy was just as happy as I was to forget the whole thing, for all she said was, "Yeah, well, I don't know. I just think you're letting a lot of guys take advantage of you."

"But why shouldn't I be friends with boys as well as girls?" I asked. "Just because I don't flirt outrageously like Marcy Cummings, does that automatically mean I'm a tomboy or just one of the guys?"

"It's not that black and white, Annie," Kathy said seriously. "At least I don't think it is. I think there's something in the middle between being good ol' Annie and a flirt."

"Like what?" I heard the challenge in my own voice. "Hanging on to every single word that comes out of Kurt Mauer's mouth?" I was already acting snippy again, in spite of my good intentions.

But to my surprise, Kathy didn't turn on me. She just smiled mysteriously. "Something like that," she said. "There's a difference between being feminine and being a flirt, and I don't think you've got to be a simpering sexpot like Marcy Cummings to make boys remember you're a girl. I also think you can be a friend without being a pal, if you know what I mean."

"I don't," I said stubbornly, even though I knew perfectly well what she meant.

"Well, look at Judy Carney," she pressed. "Do you think she's going to have a date for the Soph Hop?"

I couldn't pretend I didn't know what she meant by that. Judy Carney had always been the class tomboy, and back when we were in fifth and sixth grade, all the girls had been jealous of her because she was always tagged by the boys for their baseball teams or was asked to go along on hiking and fishing expeditions.

But that was back in grade school. The thing was, Judy Carney hadn't changed. She still came to school in patched jeans and sweatshirts, wearing no makeup, her hair cut short, and she was more interested in batting averages and carburetors than hairstyles and high heels. And the boys didn't seem to think she was the greatest anymore. They treated her almost like an outcast.

"I'm hardly like Judy Carney," I said stiffly. "I don't think that's fair, Kathy."

"Oh, *I* know you're not like her, Annie. But do *they*? Don't you see what I mean? If all the boys start looking at you as one of them, they'll stop seeing you as a real live girl. You'll never get a date."

"And you will?" I asked spitefully, mad at her because she was taking my apology and using it to lecture me.

"As a matter of fact, I *did*," she answered, sounding more amused than annoyed by my needling. "Kurt just asked me to go to the dance with him." She giggled. "So I must be doing something right."

"That's just swell, Kathy," I said. "But if you don't mind, I'd just as soon go on being myself instead of trying to be you." I didn't mean a word of it, though, and I almost confessed my crush on Tim to her, but I didn't. I couldn't. If things didn't work out between us and if Kathy, of all people, knew, I would die of embarrassment.

Kathy turned to go inside then, giving her head a little shake to show me she'd given up trying to get through to me. "You've got to do what you think is best, Annie," she said, and she didn't sound mad at all, just sort of resigned and disappointed. "But are you really being you? Because if you are, it's a side of you I've never seen before."

With that, she turned and went into the auditorium. I watched from the doorway as she walked confidently down the aisle to where Kurt was sitting. He looked as if he were listening to every word Miss Phillips, the drama coach, was saying, but I saw by the way he craned his head as Kathy came down the aisle that he'd really just been watching and waiting for her. And the warm smile he gave her as she sat down next to him made me want to cry. Kurt's smile said more than

54

Kathy had with her earnest speech. It said that she was very much a girl in his eyes, and a girl he wanted to get to know a lot better.

I trudged up the steps to my locker and got my books and coat, feeling annoyed with Kathy but knowing at the same time it wasn't really her fault that my whole day had been ruined.

For once, I was relieved that Tim wasn't waiting for me out front. Some days he still rode his bike to school, and this had clearly been one of them. I felt as if I needed time to think. But what was there to think about? I'd found my new identity, and changing it wouldn't be easy.

Besides, in my heart of hearts, I refused to believe Kathy could be right. I knew Tim liked me more than ever before. He did, he really did. And since we were friends now, surely it was just a matter of time, I thought, before we became more than that.

I pushed Kathy's words out of my mind, concentrating instead on what I'd wear to the dance when Tim invited me. I couldn't let myself consider the fact that he might not. After all, he'd already said he'd never met a girl he could talk to the way he talked to me, so who else would he ask?

By the time I got home, I'd whipped myself up to a fever of nervous anticipation. I could hardly wait to see the faces of the girls when I walked into the gym next Saturday night with Tim O'Hara next to me. Then they'd see how much Annie Wainwright knew about getting a guy!

Chapter Five

When I spotted Tim lounging around by the front entrance of school the next afternoon, I actually tingled with excitement. From the way his eyes slyly roamed the corridors while he pretended to check out the notices on the bulletin board, I could tell he was waiting for someone but trying to appear as if he weren't. And I couldn't help but hope he was waiting for me.

"Oh, hi, Annie!" he said when I was practically standing on his toes, as if he hadn't seen me coming. "What's up?"

"Not much. I was just heading home. Do you have basketball practice?"

He shook his head, moving his stack of books from one hip to the other. "Nope. Not tonight."

That was all he said. I stood there, feeling like the "old" me—tongue-tied and clumsy. Then, just when I'd decided he wasn't going to walk home with me—that he was waiting for somebody else—he made a big production of clearing his throat. "Look, Annie, do you have time to go over to Pop's and grab a Coke?"

Did I ever! "Sure, Tim, I'd love to," I told him, not even trying to sound indifferent now. Maybe going to Pop's after school wasn't exactly a big date, but it was a start. Boy, I thought, was Kathy ever wrong to try to lecture me about how to attract boys!

As we left the school grounds, taking the left turn that led to the highway and Pop's Pizzeria instead of walking straight ahead toward Polk Street, Tim was quiet as if he had something on his mind. I could just bet what it was, I thought, feeling pleased with myself and a little smug. He was going to ask me to the dance while we were at Pop's. I could feel it in my bones, and just knowing made me walk a little faster than usual because I was so eager to hear him say the words.

"Getting chilly, isn't it?" Tim mumbled as we turned the corner and neared the little red-brick pizza parlor.

"It's what my mother calls 'real fall weather.' " I told him.

"As if there's such a thing as fake fall weather!" he joked. Of course I laughed as if it were the funniest thing I'd ever heard. I was just bubbling over with good feelings. Nothing, I thought as Tim held the door open for me and we walked into Pop's, could get me down now.

I sat across from Tim at one of the little red Formica booths for two and inhaled luxuriously. "Mmm, it always smells so good in here," I murmured, reveling in the scent of tomatoes, oregano, garlic, and pepperoni.

"Want a slice?"

"Oh, no, I'm not hungry," I said quickly, embarrassed that he thought I was hinting for him to buy me something. "I'll just have a Coke."

Tim got up and went to the counter to get them while I ducked my head down and angled my compact inside my purse so I could see myself in the mirror. My blusher had worn off during the afternoon, but the crispness of the outdoors had left my cheeks pink and glowing, and I decided I looked all right.

Should I offer to pay for my Coke? I wondered as Tim headed back with two of them. I must have looked as if I were fumbling in my bag for my wallet because he sat back down across from me and said, "Here you go, Annie. These are on me."

"Thanks, Tim." I hoped I sounded as if boys buying me Cokes was just an ordinary thing. I immediately began drinking my Coke so I wouldn't have to be the first to talk. If Tim had the dance on his mind, I didn't want to drag him into some other conversation.

"I should have done this a long time ago," he said, raising his own drink in a little toast to me. "It's the least I can do to thank you for all the help you've given me."

"Oh, Tim, it was nothing," I murmured, feeling suddenly shy now that I'd finally gotten him in a sort of halfway dating situation. I looked up at him, and my heart melted. He was so adorable, with his crinkly green eyes and crooked smile. For a second I wondered what he'd do if I reached across the table and pushed the little shock of dark hair off his forehead or gently touched the scattered freckles on the bridge of his nose.

I guess I must have grinned at the total absurdity of the idea—I'd never have the nerve to do either of those things—because Tim's voice suddenly broke into my thoughts, making me jump guiltily. "What are you smiling at?" he asked, amused.

"Oh—" I said quickly, "I—I was just thinking that I was glad I could help." I wished I could talk to him without sounding like a teacher.

"Actually, I wanted to ask you something else." He got very busy all of a sudden, staring down at the table top, his fingers busily shredding the wrapper from his straw. "You know the Soph Hop's coming up next weekend," he said slowly, carefully sweeping up the little bits of ripped paper and dumping them into the ashtray.

"The Soph Hop? Oh, sure," I answered, scarcely daring to breathe. I felt as if I'd turned into two people at once—the Annie Wainwright sitting there with Tim, waiting to be asked to the dance, and another Annie Wainwright, who was across the room watching the whole thing happening, mentally jotting down every

61

word that was said, every expression that crossed Tim's face, to remember later.

"Well, do you think a guy should ask a girl to go with him even if he's not sure she'll say yes?"

He still wouldn't look me in the eye, and I was practically bursting with tenderness for him. I couldn't imagine anything cuter than what Tim was doing now, hinting around to see if I was interested in being his date before coming straight out and asking me.

His awkwardness made me feel sophisticated, and I even laughed a little as I said, "I think everyone should do what he wants. None of us knows what somebody's going to say without giving him or her a chance to say it."

"But what if the girl is someone who could probably go with practically any guy in the class?" he asked, meeting my eyes now and looking serious.

"I'm sure she'd rather go with you than anyone else," I said softly. "You should ask her, Tim."

"Maybe you're right." He reached over and squeezed my hand, and my heart started racing with happiness. He was going to ask me right now!

I stared at him as he inhaled deeply. Then he pushed back his empty soda glass. "I'll call her as soon as I get home. Thanks, Annie, you really helped me make up my mind."

"Ask her? Ask who?" I hoped he couldn't hear the awful quaver in my voice or see the color drain out of my face.

"Gee, I didn't tell you who it was, did I?" Tim said, an odd smile on his lips. "Now I'll really feel like a fool if she says no. I'm going to ask Marcy Cummings." He sighed. "I hope she doesn't already have a date."

"Marcy?" I whispered. "Oh, Tim, she'd— she'd probably love to go with you."

I reached down for the books I'd flung on the seat beside me so he couldn't see my face. I knew I looked disappointed, and I could feel hot tears of pain and humiliation filling my eyes. Boy, was the laugh ever on me! I'd been sitting here working on my acceptance speech, when all the time Tim hadn't been talking about me at all. And of all the girls for him to want to date, it *would* have to be that worm, Marcy Cummings. A lot I knew about boys!

Having to walk home with Tim after our so-called date was the worst kind of torture. I heard myself babbling on and on about the basketball team, about how great Kathy was going to be in *Our Town*, about the new ice skates I was planning to buy when the water froze in the old pond—anything to keep him from mentioning Marcy Cummings's name again.

And yet all the time I was talking, it was almost as if I weren't there at all. Something deep inside me felt dead and numbed, as lonely as the streets in the late-afternoon dusk. I never had liked twilight.

Tim seemed quiet and preoccupied on the walk home, but maybe that was just because I was rattling on so fast he didn't see much point in trying to talk. When we got to the front walk by his house, I felt a little better than I had when he'd dropped his bombshell at Pop's. That's how glad I was to be getting away from him at last.

"Thanks for your opinion, Annie," Tim said tonelessly when we came to the drive that led to the O'Haras'. He patted me on the back, the way he'd done several times before, and this time I was astounded that I'd ever let myself think there was some romantic meaning behind it. "You're a real pal, Annie."

"Thanks, Tim," I mumbled. Then, realizing how depressed I sounded, I added cheerfully, "And good luck with the dance."

"I'll see you there!" he called back as he strode up the driveway toward the house.

Did Tim really think I'd have a date for the dance? I wondered miserably as I dragged myself down the street. If he did, he was an idiot.

The truth of Kathy's warning came crashing down around my head. I knew I'd been crazy to have thought even for a minute that Tim O'Hara had asked me to the pizza shop so he could invite me to the dance. And I knew I had about as much chance of being asked by some other boy as I did of becoming the Queen Mother.

All this time I thought I was being so smart, but I'd never suspected that the game I was playing was a losing one. Tim had called me a "real pal," and I was beginning to see all too clearly that "pals" didn't get asked to dances.

But how come flirts like Marcy Cummings did? That's what I couldn't understand. I didn't resent Kathy going with Kurt. After all, she was an open, genuine sort of person. But phony Marcy Cummings? What did *she* have to offer anybody? Why did Tim like her better than me? What was *I* doing that was such a dreadful turn-off?

I pulled my shoulders back and kept my chin straight as I walked up the path to my front door. If Tim could fall for some airhead like Marcy Cummings, I told myself, it was probably just as well we weren't going out together. Any boy who could fall for Marcy couldn't possibly be interested in me.

If the way Marcy acted was the only way to get a guy interested, I vowed as I hung up my jacket and bounded up the stairs to my room that I'd never go out on a date in my life and I'd be proud of it.

That's what I told myself. But I didn't feel proud. Or happy. I felt jealous, mean, envious, and hurt. I'd never liked Marcy, but right then, I hated her with a passion. Because, terrible as she was, Tim O'Hara didn't think of her as a "pal." If I could have changed places with her for just one week, I knew I'd have jumped at the chance.

Chapter Six

I don't know how Mom and Dad managed to sit through dinner with me that night. For once in my life, I was thankful that my folks were naturally untalkative. It made my silence a bit less noticeable. I picked halfheartedly at my chicken à la king, pushing it around on its bed of rice more than eating it, and I couldn't finish my dessert.

"You're not coming down with a cold, are you, dear?" Mom asked when I'd pushed my dessert plate back with most of the cake still on it. She reached over and gently laid the back of her hand across my forehead, then shook her head. "No, you don't feel warm."

"I'm OK," I insisted. "I just ate a big lunch today."

Mom nodded briskly, as if to say that settled that. "I'm afraid you're going to have to do the dishes alone tonight, Annie," she said, changing the subject. "Your father and I promised Aunt Maude we'd stop by to visit, and I know how bored you get at her house."

I nodded. "No problem." I felt so lonely it was almost better to be all by myself.

Heaven knew I couldn't have put up with Aunt Maude tonight, I mused while I scraped the dishes and rinsed them before setting them in the dishwasher.

Aunt Maude wasn't really an aunt. She was my dad's great aunt or third cousin once removed or something like that, and he'd spent a lot of time with her when he was growing up, since Aunt Maude had never married and had lived with his parents.

I never felt comfortable around Aunt Maude. She was so old and fossilized I felt as if she belonged to the Ice Age. And she didn't seem to know how to act around a teenage girl. She treated Mom and me as if we were the same age. I guess to her we were all just young people.

Tonight as I wiped off the dining room table, I felt sorrier for Aunt Maude than I ever had before. A tear even trickled down my cheek as I wondered if Aunt Maude had been a "pal" to the boys back in the good old days when she was a girl.

The phone rang, jerking me out of my doldrums, and I couldn't help smiling to myself as I went to answer it. Fifteen was still pretty young to be considered a spinster, I reminded myself. I was getting as dramatic as Kathy!

"Hi, Annie," she said when I answered the phone, just as if I'd conjured her up.

"Oh, Kathy, hello." I plopped down on one of the chairs at the kitchen table. I hoped she hadn't called to rub in the fact that Kurt had asked her to the dance. Not that I'd blame her if she had. Now that I realized she'd been right, I could see she'd been trying to talk to me for my own good. But I didn't want her to know that yet.

"You busy?" she asked.

"Sort of. Mom and Dad went out, and I've got a slew of dishes to wash," I explained, even though the dishes were already nestled in the washer. "I can talk for a minute, though," I added, not wanting Kathy to get mad at me all over again. "How was rehearsal today?"

"Oh, it was good. It's going to be an excellent production, I think. But I wish they hadn't scheduled it just two weeks after the Soph Hop. With the dance just a week away, some of these girls can't even concentrate on their lines." She sounded disgusted. "You'd think they'd never had a date in their lives."

Like me, I thought. Only, this time I might not have a date, either. "That'll be all over by next week," I reminded her. "Then everyone should be able to concentrate again."

"Everybody but Marcy Cummings," she said pointedly, and I physically cringed. If there was any name I didn't feel like hearing, it was hers. I couldn't say anything, but Kathy didn't wait for my comments before going on. "The way she's been acting lately, you'd think she got the role of Emily instead of just the understudy. I swear I wouldn't be surprised if she poisoned Janice Larson just so she could go on instead."

"Oh, Kathy, she can't be that bad," I insisted, but I couldn't keep the pleasure out of my voice. I was thrilled that Kathy still disliked Marcy just as much as I did.

"Maybe not." Her voice sounded grudging. "But she makes me sick sometimes. And now the worst thing in the world has happened!"

"What's that?" I asked, hoping we could get the conversation away from Marcy.

I should have known better. Kathy lowered her voice as if she didn't want anyone else in the house to overhear her. "I know it's hard to believe, but my half-wit brother just told me he'd asked Marcy to the dance. Isn't that unreal? I mean, I thought the poor boy had a little taste. I've already told him not to expect to double date with Kurt and me."

"You—you mean she accepted?"

"Of course she did. I always knew Marcy would do anything for a date with Tim. Or with anyone else on one of the teams, for that matter. I just thought Tim had a little more sense than to fall for someone like her."

"Maybe Tim likes sugar and spice and everything nice," I suggested lightly.

"Sugar and spice!" she snorted. "How about saccharin? C'mon, Annie, you know as well as I do that Marcy Cummings is about as cuddly as a rattlesnake. Anyhow, I know I came down on you for giving the guys advice, but I thought maybe you could talk to Tim. He seems to respect your opinion. Maybe if you tried to tell him what a viper Marcy is, he'd listen. I just don't want my brother getting hung up on a creature like that. Tim and I may fight a lot, but he's still my twin, and I'd hate to see her get her claws into him."

"No, I couldn't, Kathy." I didn't say anything for a minute, genuinely trying to decide how I felt about it. All I knew was that trying to talk Tim out of Marcy would just make a bad situation worse. Advice was one thing. Nagging was another.

"How come?"

"For starters, because it's none of my business. For another, if Tim likes Marcy, there's nothing I could say that would change it. And for another, I—I kind of like Tim, Kathy—don't you dare tell anyone—and it wouldn't look so hot if I tried to turn him off from Marcy and then expected to go out with him myself."

"Annie, you didn't tell me—"

"I know," I said quickly, cutting her off. "I don't quite know what to do about it."

I heard her sigh. "I don't either," she

72

said finally, "but maybe we're making too much out of the whole thing. I mean, it shouldn't take more than one date for Tim to find out what a catty little monster she is beneath that sweet front."

All of a sudden I knew that if I had to listen to one more word about Tim and Marcy I'd scream. "Well, I'd better go," I said. "By the way, do you want to go to the church flea market with me next Saturday? Mom says it's supposed to be good—lots of books and records and food and stuff."

"Sure. I've got a few extra dollars. But I won't be able to stay long. You know, because of the dance and all."

"Oh, sure." I couldn't keep a touch of sarcasm out of my voice. "You've got to have plenty of time to get ready for the dance."

I guess Kathy had been so busy being excited about going with Kurt to the dance that she hadn't thought much about the fact that I would be dateless. Now I heard the intake of her breath as it hit her. "Don't worry, Annie," she assured me, "somebody'll ask you."

"I couldn't care less about going to some dumb sophomore dance," I snapped. "It's not as if it's the prom or anything, Kathy." And *that* rang so phony in my own ears that I decided I'd better hang up quickly. "Look, I've really got to go. I'll talk to you later."

After I'd replaced the receiver, I stormed around the house, banging the kitchen cupboards closed and slamming the dishwasher shut so hard I was afraid I'd broken the plates. If there was one thing I didn't need in my life, it was to have my best friend feeling sorry for me! So what if I didn't have a date for the Soph Hop? All the other guys probably took it for granted that Tim was taking me, I told myself. After all, they'd seen us together enough. And if Tim O'Hara's idea of a date was Marcy Cummings, I'd rather be an old maid like Aunt Maude any day!

My mood was so bad I couldn't concentrate on TV or anything, and I didn't feel like seeing Mom and Dad when they got in, not while I was practically breathing fire. So I stomped upstairs to my room and, sitting cross-legged on the floor, started rearranging all the books and records on the wall of white shelves opposite my twin beds. I knew I was in such a state I had to channel my energy and do something constructive. What I really felt like doing was tearing the room apart.

By the time Saturday rolled around, I'd almost convinced myself I didn't care about the dance. I pushed it so far into the back of my mind I actually managed to have a good time at the church bazaar. It was just Kathy and me together like in the old days, before we'd cared about boys and dates. We wandered from booth to booth in the big church basement, trying on old hats and rummaging through secondhand record albums, magazines, and books.

We left with treasures: I'd found two old Beatles albums I'd been wanting, and a white, lace-trimmed lamp for the table next to my bed. Kathy had snatched up an old pink feather boa, saying, "It clashes hideously with my hair, and it's taking a huge chunk out of my allowance, but I've got to have it! Just picture me opening night, trailing my boa behind me! I'll be so glamorous, I could die!"

That was the old Kathy, the Kathy who lived more in her fantasies of starring on Broadway than in draping herself all over Kurt Mauer. As we huddled together in the cold bus, I couldn't help but wish we'd never grown up. Life certainly had been simpler back in grade school.

But I didn't really start getting depressed until after dinner. My appetite had disappeared, even though I'd had nothing to eat all day except a burger and Coke at the church sale, and I left the table with my roast beef and mashed potatoes barely touched.

"Aren't you and Kathy going to the movies or anything tonight, Annie?" my mother asked when I excused myself.

"No, not tonight. She's got to practice her scenes for the class play," I lied.

When I was safely closeted in my bedroom, I wondered, now, why in the world did I do that to Mom? But I knew the answer. I didn't want my parents to know there was a dance at the school that I wasn't going to. And I didn't much like admitting it to myself either.

Mom and Dad must have thought it was weird that I was a sophomore and still didn't have boys hanging around the house. I knew from looking through old family albums that Mom had been very popular when she was my age. There were lots of photos of her looking not that much different than she did now, except for her funny fifties' poodle skirt and long sack dresses, and in a lot of the pictures, teenage boys with crew cuts and duck tails were standing or sitting beside her.

If she ever tried to figure out why I wasn't Miss Popularity, she kept it to herself. Maybe, like me, she had figured I was a late bloomer who would blossom into a girl boys liked as soon as I got rid of the baby fat. But did she wonder why I had no guys calling on the phone now that I was thin?

Of course, Marcy Cummings was thin, too.

That thought popped into my mind as if it had been sent by the devil himself. And once I started thinking about Marcy, I couldn't stop. Slumping against the pillows I'd propped on the headboard of my bed, I tried to concentrate on the old album spinning on the turntable, but all I could think of was Marcy Cummings whirling around the floor of the gym in Tim O'Hara's arms, craning her neck to look up at him and making her eyes extra wide in that affected way of hers, giggling and cooing and murmuring in his ear in the hushed, breathy voice she put on only for a boy.

I wouldn't let myself be like her, I vowed.

I just wouldn't! Not even if it meant never having a date as long as I lived. But maybe Kathy's view of the situation was more accurate than I liked to admit, I thought grudgingly. Maybe I should keep my mouth shut from now on and stop helping all the guys sort out their lives. What was the point if I just ended up hurt and miserable?

From now on, I decided, I would ignore Tim O'Hara. If he wanted to talk, we could talk about me. Or about classes or sports or movies. Anything but his troubles. "When he's got a problem, he can go to the guidance counselor!" I hissed out loud.

That didn't make me feel any better, though. How could I feel the slightest bit happy when I knew practically everybody else in the sophomore class was having a great time at the Castle Heights High Soph Hop?

I took a long, hot bath, filling the tub with Mom's best perfumed bath oil. Afterward, I put my bathrobe on over my flannel pajamas and tiptoed very quietly down the stairs and into the kitchen. I didn't want Mom and Dad to hear me.

Feeling like a criminal, I filled a big bowl with chocolate ice cream, piled a plate with oatmeal cookies, and snuck it all back to my room to drown my sorrows in self-indulgence.

Even that didn't help. I went to bed feeling worse than ever, knowing perfectly well that if I started consoling myself by pigging out in secret, I'd be a butterball again in no time. And then I'd probably have an even smaller chance of getting a boyfriend—even if I learned every little trick in Marcy Cummings's sneaky mind!

Chapter Seven

Midterms started a little more than a week after the dance, so I didn't have much time to mope around about Tim. I was too busy studying for tests and writing reports to wonder how he was doing with Marcy, though I could tell they were definitely an item from the number of times I'd seen them in the halls together.

Looking back now, I realize how depressed I was then, but at the time I didn't let myself see it, because I worried that my preoccupation with boys in general, and Tim in particular, would have a bad effect on my grades.

I didn't feel especially upset when I spotted Tim and Marcy together because I'd sort of given up. I'd decided that if Marcy was Tim's ideal, I was out of the running. I considered myself lucky just to be his friend, and I concentrated on geometry and French verbs and history.

The one bright spot during those weeks was the sophomore class play. Since Marcy was an understudy, she had to sit through the whole thing backstage—undoubtedly praying that "Emily" would break her leg before the last act and she'd have a chance to star in at least part of *Our Town*. The only consolation I had was that I didn't have to watch her snuggling up to Tim, who was seated with his parents two rows in front of where I sat with Carole Deutsch.

Kathy was terrific as always, and as Carole and I were leaving to meet some other kids at Pop's, we ran into her in the hallway, her eyes shining. She'd already changed for the party, and she really did look chic, almost glamorous, in a pretty dress of ice-blue wool, with the beloved boa trailing across her shoulders.

"You were wonderful, Kathy," I congratulated her, giving her a big hug.

She giggled. "What do you think of my evening clothes?" she kidded.

"That boa's something else!" Carole told her. "Where in the world did you get it?"

"Oh, a very *exclusive* little boutique." She caught my eye and winked. "Thank goodness my hair was sprayed gray to play the mother! Otherwise, the pink and red would clash so badly you'd both be blinded." She craned her neck, checking to see who else was milling around the corridor in front of the auditorium. "I've got to run and find Mom and Dad before the party," she said. "Why don't you both drop by the house in about an hour? Mom baked a cake, and she's going to serve some punch and stuff."

"That sounds great!" Carole turned to me. "How about it, Annie?"

I yawned. "Oh, I don't think so," I said, feeling suddenly drained of energy. "I'm getting sleepy already—it must be an aftereffect from studying so hard for midterms. But I'll walk you to Kathy's, Carole," I added. "It's on my way home from Pop's."

"I really think you should come over, Annie," Kathy said pointedly, but I forced another yawn before smiling at her brightly.

"No, no, thanks," I said quickly. And then, "You really were good. Have a great time at

82

the party. And tell Kurt I thought he was wonderful, too."

I felt sly, and very pleased with myself. The mere mention of Kurt's name was enough to make Kathy forget about my problems. "Wasn't he? Next time he should be the leading man, though," she said seriously. "I mean, he's much too handsome to be made up like an old man."

With a quick, "I hope you change your mind and come, Annie," she dashed away, and Carole and I headed toward Pop's, part of a long procession of kids going that way for Cokes and pizza.

"Are you sure you don't want to stop at the O'Haras' for just a minute, Annie?" Carole asked when we were leaving, about an hour later.

I shook my head firmly. "No, I can't. I'm so exhausted I'd just be a drag. I can hardly wait to get home and fall into bed."

Not until I'd said goodbye to Carole at the O'Haras' driveway and continued on by myself did I admit to myself the real reason I didn't want to go to Kathy's house: I just couldn't face seeing Tim with Marcy Cummings, looking at her the way I longed to have him look at me.

Then just a few days later I had to face a difficult and rather embarrassing situation. I hadn't spoken much with Tim since that day he'd asked me to Pop's, and for some reason, I took it for granted that he wouldn't be asking me for help with his problems anymore. So when I noticed him lurking at the cafeteria entrance at lunchtime one day, I didn't think anything of it. Instead, I thought how cute he looked in his corduroys and kelly-green sweater, which brought out the green of his eyes and made his hair look even blacker than black. I caught my breath, but I didn't let myself get carried away. Anyway, he was probably just waiting for Marcy.

"Hi, Tim," I said coolly as I started to push open the swinging doors.

To my surprise, he grabbed my elbow, stopping me. "Wait, Annie," he said. "You meeting anyone?"

I stared in surprise. "Well, no, not really." I wondered what he was getting at. "Why?"

"Would you like to go to Pop's and split a submarine with me?"

"Pop's?" My voice practically cracked. I mean, even though we were allowed off campus for lunch, hardly anybody but seniors ever really took advantage of it.

"Sure, why not? We can get there, eat, and be back in an hour if we hustle." He smiled his irresistible half-shy, half-cocky smile. "I'll even treat you to your half."

A little voice in my head (my pride, maybe?) was whispering, "Tell him no." But the thought of being with Tim, of sitting at a table and talking to him, was too strong. As if a ventriloquist were making my mouth work, I heard myself mumbling, "Sure. Just let me get my coat."

When I met him by the front door a few minutes later, he was as bundled up as I was, the collar of his blue-and-gold basketball jacket pulled up against the November winds.

"Looks like we'll have snow before Thanksgiving," he predicted. We trudged along toward Pop's, keeping our heads down as the blast of biting air brought tears to our eyes and numbed our cheeks.

"I'd better shake the mothballs out of all my sweaters," I said, keeping up my wall of coolness. (What I wanted to do was grab his arm and say, "Tim, please tell me what I did wrong!") We rounded a corner, and a gust of wind swept through the bare trees with such strength that I gasped. Neither of us spoke after that. We just concentrated on getting inside the pizza parlor as soon as possible.

But despite the cold, I felt pretty warm and cozy inside. Not even the leaden sky could take the edge off my high spirits, and I realized how much I'd missed Tim recently.

We made small talk as Tim sliced the meatball hoagie in half, and then we ate hungrily, laughing as the tomato sauce dripped onto the table. I didn't want this hour to end, but I knew it had to. And I wasn't any fool—I also knew Tim had asked me there for a reason and that it probably wasn't the reason I was hoping for.

Finally, to my dismay, he got around to the subject I'd been dreading. "I guess you know by now that Marcy and I went to the Soph Hop," he said casually, not knowing, of course, that I'd thought of practically nothing else ever since.

"Did you have a nice time?" I asked, hearing my voice come out all rigid and chilly.

"Sure, a great time, really great," he answered quickly. I thought he sounded a little too enthusiastic.

I bet Marcy flirted with every boy there, I thought, but I didn't say anything. I just sat there and smiled, hoping he couldn't see that I was jealous and hurting inside.

"I kind of thought we'd run into you there," Tim said, raising his eyebrows curiously and focusing those green eyes on me as if he expected a comment.

What did he expect me to say? That I'd wanted to go with him and nobody else had asked me? "Oh, well, I had something else I had to do," I said weakly.

"What do you think of Marcy, Annie?" Tim asked suddenly. "I mean, you've known her a long time and everything, right?"

I was speechless. Why on earth was Tim asking me for my opinion of that creep? I opened my mouth to say I couldn't stand her, but then I slammed it shut. If Tim was hung up on her and I put her down, I'd be the loser. He would think I was just jealous if I said what I really thought. (Well, face it, I *was* jealous, and it probably would show if I said anything bad about her.)

I wrestled with my thoughts and finally just slouched down a little farther in the booth and said as blandly as possible, "She's all right, I guess. We've never exactly been part of the same crowd."

"Yeah, she said she was always sort of

old for her age." He announced it as if it were an accomplishment, like she'd won the Nobel Prize. Old for her age! If old meant stuck-up, affected, back-stabbing and gossipy, she certainly was old for her age! I was too mad to comment, afraid all the hateful things in my mind would spill out of my mouth if I opened it. So I just shrugged.

"But she's terrific when you get to know her," he went on, perhaps guessing Marcy wasn't exactly my favorite person. "It's hard to believe she's shy, isn't it? She says sometimes she's so scared of people, she can hardly talk."

I almost choked on my ginger ale at that one. Marcy Cummings shy! She was about as shy as a nest of wasps and just as deadly. I could imagine what she'd told Tim—that she was quiet and fragile and needed a big, strong basketball player to protect her. It made me want to throw up.

"See, Annie, she says that because she has so much trouble talking to people she doesn't think she should get tied down to just one boy when she's just a sophomore." I perked up at that, then immediately felt guilty, seeing that Tim looked miserable. "She says it's not fair of me to expect her not to date other guys just because we're going out. But I'm not the kind of guy who likes playing the field." He sighed, running his fingers through his hair and looking so lost I wanted to throw my arms around him and tell him everything would be all right. But then he said, "So what I wondered was, what do you think I should do, Annie? You've always given me such good advice."

I couldn't talk for a second. It was all so weird that I felt as if I were dreaming—or having a nightmare, to be exact. Anytime now, I'd wake up and be in my bed, not here at Pop's with Tim sitting across from me waiting for me to tell him what to do about Marcy.

The worst part was that I couldn't possibly tell him what I really thought. So I stalled for time, draining the last of my ginger ale and trying to figure out what I could say that wouldn't make Tim hate me forever. Finally I murmured, "You've got to do what you think is best, Tim."

Then, hoping he'd take the hint, I pulled on my coat and stood up. "Look at the time. We better make a run for it, or we'll be late for class."

But he wouldn't give up. It was too cold and windy to talk as we dashed back to school, but as soon as we were inside the front door, he turned to me and said, just as if we'd never stopped the conversation, "So you think I should just be patient with Marcy and not try to push her into going steady?"

The only place I thought Marcy should be pushed was over the edge of a cliff, but I could hardly tell Tim that. So I just nodded. "Sure, Tim. No girl likes to be pressured, you know."

Tim squeezed my hand so hard it almost hurt. "You're a gem! I don't know what I'd do without you, Annie."

"Thanks for lunch," I somehow whispered as I headed for my locker. Tim would never know that my lunch felt as if it had rolled itself into a hard little ball in my stomach. I walked away with a big smile pasted on, refusing to let my feelings show. But all that anger building up in me needed some release, and after I'd hung up my coat and scarf and grabbed my books, I slammed my locker door so hard people turned to stare.

What was wrong with me? I wondered miserably. I was practically going out of my way to make myself feel worse. The last thing in the world I wanted was to see Tim get even more involved with Marcy. But I was trapped by my own image. I'd given Tim such "good" advice before that he was relying on me. And I knew I couldn't expose my real feelings about Marcy without giving away how I felt about him myself.

I drifted through the rest of the afternoon in a daze, mad at myself and just as mad at Tim. I blamed him for falling for such a phony in the first place, and I blamed myself for not being able to talk to him without playing "Dear Annie."

But I was in a real bind. I couldn't give up spending time with Tim. And even though I hated to admit it, I knew I was scared he cared about me only as long as I could help him out. And having him depend on me for advice, as terrible as it was, was better than not having him around at all.

Chapter Eight

The next few weeks were unbearable. Not even the big turkey and the pumpkin pie Mom made for Thanksgiving could lift my spirits.

Basketball season was in full swing, and I couldn't stay away from the games. I'd go with Carole and Kathy—when she didn't have a date with Kurt—and my eyes would be glued to Tim the entire time, whether he was on the court or sitting on the sidelines. And try as I might, I couldn't make myself stop staring at Marcy, who always sat in one of the front rows, batting her eyes and smiling sweetly whenever Tim looked her way.

When the games were over, I'd try to think of an excuse to go straight home instead of joining the kids at Pop's. I just couldn't stand having to watch Marcy cling to Tim.

If it hadn't been for my work for the newspaper and the fact that our schoolwork was getting more demanding all the time, I think I might have gone totally crazy. Tim still sought my company, and that was the worst part, because as often as not he wanted advice on his relationship with Marcy, and I simply could not tell him I thought the only way to handle her was with a ten-foot pole.

So anytime our conversation turned to Marcy, I'd be mumbling dumb things like "You've got to follow your heart" or "You can't pay attention to what anyone else thinks." I knew I had to say something, so I compromised by keeping my comments bland enough to be almost unnoticeable. I wasn't enough of a hypocrite to actually *praise* Marcy, but I never once let Tim guess how much I really disliked the girl.

In the meantime, Kathy and Kurt started going steady, and I felt lonelier and more forlorn than ever. I started studying Kathy, trying to figure out how she could be so down-to-earth and have a boyfriend, too. In my case, being down-to-earth meant being one of the guys, and not a single guy in the sophomore class of Castle Heights High School seemed interested in asking me out.

I must have been acting pretty weird, for one December afternoon, when we were sitting around the fireplace in the O'Haras' basement rec room, Kathy asked, "What's been bothering you, Annie?"

I looked up from the marshmallow I was roasting. "Why?"

"It's just the way I catch you staring at me lately—like I was a bug under a microscope or something," she said. "It's creepy. And I figured you wouldn't look at me that way unless you were mad at me or something."

"Don't be silly. I'm not looking at you any differently than I usually do," I fibbed.

"Is it Tim and Marcy?" Kathy asked.

I looked at the floor and didn't say anything.

"You know, maybe now's the time to do something about it," she said. "Maybe you haven't been aggressive enough."

"But I can't just jump in between them," I said.

"I know, but at least let Tim see how terrific you are. Don't *hide* from him."

Before I could answer that, we both heard high-pitched giggling coming from upstairs as the front door slammed shut. Kathy rolled her eyes in disgust. "Tim's brought her over again." She groaned. "Oh, Annie, how awful for you. Look, maybe I'll have a long talk with my dear brother soon. That creep is just leading him on. And you're certainly not feeling terrific about it."

I smiled gratefully at her, then heard the two of them clumping down the stairs. I stood up. "I've got to go," I told Kathy.

"OK," she said. "I understand."

"Hey, everybody," Tim called, bounding down the last few steps and as usual sort of taking my breath away. "You're not leaving already, are you, Annie?"

"I've got to study," I stammered.

And there she was, behind him, her hand possessively on his shoulder, her voice dripping with syrupy sweetness. "Why, I'll bet you study a lot, don't you, Annie?" she asked, snickering just in case I missed the point.

"Oh, only when I'm not nightclubbing or having tea with the prime minister or something," I said lightly. There was no way I was going to let her get to me.

Tim let loose with a big laugh, which he

probably would have kept to himself if he'd seen the way Marcy's lips tightened into a thin line in back of him.

I gave her an extra-sweet smile, very close to my Movie Star Smile, as I backed toward the stairs. "See you all tomorrow."

Of course, Marcy ruined my dignified exit. As I marched up the stairs, I heard her cooing, "Isn't it wonderful the way Annie's *always* studying? I wish I didn't have so many other things to keep me busy."

And I wish you'd fall in front of a school bus, I thought as I grabbed my coat and books from the table in the entrance hall and stormed out of the house.

After that, you'd think I might have gotten up the nerve to tell Tim exactly what I thought of Marcy Cummings, right? Wrong.

I couldn't. I just couldn't. I was still too scared that I'd turn him off completely if I said I didn't approve. And at the same time I hated myself for being the world's biggest hypocrite. I really did not know what to do.

I reached what I guess you'd call the bitter end right before Christmas. Kathy had rehearsals again, this time for the New Year's Revue, and I was trudging home alone one day through grubby, week-old snow when Tim suddenly caught up with me.

"Whew!" he gasped, his cheeks red from the cold, his eyes greener than ever. "I yelled to you, but the wind must be against me." He clutched his side. "I guess I'm not in as great shape as I'd like to think. Running two blocks really winded me."

I slowed my steps so he could get his breath back, but I felt none of the happiness I'd have felt a few weeks before. So he'd raced to catch up with me. Big deal. I knew now it wasn't because he was crazy about my company.

I didn't even start a conversation. I almost didn't want to talk. If we didn't talk, I could just enjoy Tim walking along beside me. But if we did talk, I knew I'd be reminded of the two things I didn't want to think about: that I was just Tim's buddy and that Marcy Cummings was the girl he really loved.

"Going to Kenny Farrell's Christmas party?" he asked when he'd caught his breath.

I shook my head. "We're going to my grandmother's in Allentown for four days."

"Oh, that's too bad. Plenty of kids will be there, and Kenny's parents are always great about parties. They really stay out of the way."

"I'm sure I won't be missed," I mumbled, finally giving in to a little self-pity.

"Won't be missed?" He honestly sounded amazed. "You shouldn't joke about things like that, Annie. *I'll* miss you," he added, and my heart stood still until he went on, "especially since Marcy's going with Barry Goldstein."

"She's going with one of your friends?" I mean, I'd always known Marcy was low, but this was her lowest.

"Yeah." I glanced over, but he wasn't looking at me. His eyes were on the icy sidewalk. I could tell by the set of his jaw and the slump of his shoulders that he was miserable. He sighed deeply. "I guess it's not her fault. She told me she'd waited for me to ask her, and when I didn't, she accepted Barry. I guess I shouldn't have just taken for granted she'd go with me, you know?"

Of course you should have taken it for granted, I wanted to scream. *She's supposed to be your girlfriend, you dummy!*

But I didn't say that. I just sort of murmured, "Well, I guess maybe she didn't really know you were planning to ask her."

He looked up at me, and I could see relief relaxing his tense muscles. "Yeah, next time I'll know better, right?"

"Sure," I muttered, wondering why it was taking him so long to get the hint that Marcy was giving him the royal runaround. I was so fed up with him for being so stupid that I barely said another word until we got to his house. Then I just whispered, "Goodbye."

Just as I got to my house, I ran into Doug Ruffner and Kenny. "Annie, baby," Kenny said, "what's happening?"

I shrugged, then caught myself and smiled brightly. Maybe it wouldn't hurt to flirt a little with some boys.

"Actually," I said as coyly as I could manage, "I'm *miserable* because I'm going to be out of town for your Christmas party."

"You are? Not fair! Not fair!" he shouted, and I started laughing. "I'll have you arrested, I'll take you to court, no jury will listen to you!" Then he calmed down again. "Seriously, Annie, that's a drag."

"You're going to miss a great party," Doug added, grinning. "Sandy says she'd rather die than miss it."

"It's not going to be the same without you, Annie," Kenny said, sounding serious for once.

"Oh, you're just saying that," I insisted,

but secretly I was flattered. "Plenty of other girls will be there."

And then, just as I was starting to feel I might have some sort of future at Castle Heights High, he said, "Yeah, but the other girls aren't like you, Annie," he said. "I mean, you're just one of the guys."

I looked up quickly to see if he was joking, but he looked really regretful, and I realized he thought he was paying me some kind of compliment. And to make things worse, Doug was nodding in agreement.

Hot tears burned my eyes, and I turned my head so they couldn't see. "I gotta go. See you around."

"See ya, Annie," they said in unison, and as I slogged through the slush on the front walk, I turned to watch them go off, hitting each other on the arm and laughing and yelling the way boys do when they're together. Everything in me wanted to yell after them that I wasn't like that. I was not one of the guys. I was a *girl*, a girl just like any other girl!

I felt so upset and out of sorts that night that I went to bed almost as soon as we'd had dinner. I could hardly wait for Christmas vacation. I was dying to get away from Castle

Heights and everyone who looked on me as "good old Annie," the kind of girl everyone liked but no one would ever love.

When I awoke the next day, it was snowing very hard. After lunch, the principal's voice came over the loudspeaker, announcing in a tinny tone mixed with static that, because of weather conditions, school would be dismissed at one-thirty and that we should all listen to the radio the next morning to see if classes would be resumed before vacation started.

I was in English at the time, and all the kids were shouting and cheering in the way that makes teachers cringe. I was glad, too, but not glad enough to shout with happiness. I was glad because I was going to have an extra break from everybody in the sophomore class, everybody I hated for not seeing me the way I really was, for making me so confused I wasn't even sure who Annie Wainwright was anymore.

Kathy and Kurt were holding hands by the front door as I came down the corridor. The mere sight of them made me feel more cut off. I didn't think I could bear it if they expected me to walk with them—I couldn't face having to be near anyone who was happy and part of a couple—so I turned and hurried back around the corner that led downstairs to a side door.

I fought my way home through snow mixed with icy, blinding sleet, feeling something like satisfaction every time I stepped in a drift so deep I felt wetness seeping over the tops of my boots. Maybe I'd get pneumonia; then everybody would be sorry, I thought furiously. But even as I thought it, I felt like a baby, and *that* made me feel so bad that I began to cry, tears sliding down my cheeks and mixing with the wet snow.

"Thank goodness you're back," Mom said when she met me at the door. "I heard on the radio that all schools were closing early."

I let her help me out of my iced, stiff coat, too chilled and sick at heart to make conversation. "Why, you're cold as an icicle, Annie!" She laid her warm hand on my forehead. "Let me make you a cup of tea and honey so you don't catch a chill."

"Thanks, Mom," I mumbled. I followed her numbly into the kitchen and dropped onto a chair, feeling more tired and achy every second and remembering my awful wish to get sick.

Mom puttered around the kitchen, keeping up an unusually steady stream of chatter about how she hoped we wouldn't have to cancel our plans to go to Gran's house. It wasn't like her to talk so much, but then, it wasn't like me to sit there playing zombie, so maybe she guessed something was wrong. All I know is that all the attention she was paying me and all the worried looks she kept giving me only made me feel worse.

I can't explain what came over me in the kitchen while I waited for the kettle to boil. It was as if all the snow falling outside were falling on me, suffocating me and shutting me off from other people. All the way home I'd been crying because nobody cared about me, and now that Mom was absolutely hovering over me, I felt like crying all the more.

When I got my tea, I took it upstairs to my room, and Mom agreed with me that I should tuck myself in bed so I wouldn't get sick.

It was too late, though. By the time she came to wake me for dinner, every bone in my body throbbed. She took one look at my watery eyes and runny nose and shook her head. "You stay in bed, young lady, and I'll bring up a tray. You don't want to have a cold for Christmas and miss all the fun."

Fun, I thought miserably after she'd gone back downstairs, what fun? Fun was having a date and going to Kenny Farrell's party and being the kind of girl boys put an arm around without adding a big slap on the back. And that kind of fun, I thought weakly as I dozed off again, was the kind I would never have.

Chapter Nine

Well, as it turned out, I didn't catch pneumonia. I didn't even come down with an especially bad cold, just a case of the sniffles, enough to give me a good excuse to stay in bed until we left for my grandmother's. I didn't really *need* an excuse, since the snow kept coming down hard enough to make the officials decide to call off school until after the holidays. But it was just as well I didn't have to explain to Mom that I wasn't getting out of bed just because I couldn't see any reason to. My cold covered up the fact that most of my lousy feelings weren't physical.

The snow stopped the afternoon before

we were supposed to leave for Allentown. Dad still wasn't sure it was going to be safe to drive, but that night a thaw set in, and by the next day, the roads were wet but clear, with the grimy, leftover snow sloshed alongside.

Thank goodness for Gran! She could always snap me out of a bad mood. She's my mother's mother, but very different from her—smaller, and as delicate as a sparrow, always cheerful and peppy, never seeming depressed, even though she's been alone since Grandpop died five years before.

We had a real old-fashioned Christmas, and for once, I was glad to be surrounded by my family. The tree filled almost half of Gran's small living room. She popped corn to string into garlands and dug out the decorations she'd had since Mom was my age. We decorated the tree together Christmas Eve, then carefully deposited our wrapped presents under it before going to the Christmas Eve service at Gran's parish church, an ancient, doll-sized building that wasn't like any building in Castle Heights, most of which, according to Dad, dated back only as far as the 1930s.

Christmas Day dawned bright and clear and cold. We all chipped in and helped with the big midday dinner, and as usual, Gran cooked as if she were feeding an army instead of just Mom and Dad and me and my Aunt Helen and Uncle Ben, who lived down the road.

My diet went out the window that afternoon, not because I was still depressed but because everything was too yummy to pass up. There was a big turkey with giblet gravy. There were candied sweet potatoes, bread stuffing, home-baked rolls, lima beans, stewed tomatoes Gran had put up in the fall, stuffed celery sticks, pickled beets, and cranberry relish. To top it all off, we had pumpkin pie, mince pie, and Aunt Helen's special fruitcake. By the time we'd finished eating, we were too full to move, and we dawdled around the table for ages before any of us could even think of moving into the living room to start unwrapping presents.

For once, I truly loved every gift I received: the angora sweater from my aunt and uncle, the hand-knit scarf and gloves from Gran, the portable typewriter from my parents. After everything had been opened and shown around and the wrappings cleared up, Uncle Ben sat at Gran's little upright piano and played Christmas carols. We sang "Silent Night," "O Come All Ye Faithful," and all my favorites from when I was a little kid.

The only thing that made me at all sad was that I couldn't stay here and avoid going back to school and being stuck living out the part of "Dear Annie" for the rest of my high-school career. I dreaded going back to Castle Heights—even before I knew what was in store for me.

And what was in store for me was one of the biggest fights I'd ever had with Kathy. No sooner had we walked through the door and hung our coats up than the phone rang.

"It's for you, Annie," Mom called from the kitchen. "Kathy, I think."

"I'll take it in the den, Mom," I told her, closing the door behind me and settling myself on the couch.

I was all set to listen to Kathy talk about what Kurt had given her for Christmas or how terrific Kenny Farrell's party had been so I was pretty taken aback when, the second I said hello, she snapped, "Annie Wainwright, what exactly are you up to?"

"What's that supposed to mean?" I asked.

"It means I finally got my nerve up to try to talk some sense into Tim about his stupid relationship with Marcy Cummings," she said, her voice tight and cold. "And do you know what he told me?"

"No," I answered.

"Well, he told me that not everyone felt about Marcy the way I did and that I was clearly wrong about her. He told me that you just *adore* the girl and agreed with him that dear Marcy would never give him the run-around. What's the big idea?" she ended up, sounding more puzzled than mad now. "I thought you liked Tim."

"I do like Tim," I insisted. "I—I like him a lot. You know that."

"Then why in the *world* are you encouraging him to keep seeing Marcy? That's the stupidest thing I ever heard of. And not only *that*, Marcy's got him so mixed-up that his grades are slipping, and if he doesn't bring them up, Mom's going to make him quit the basketball team."

"Oh, no. How awful!" I gasped.

"You *do* remember Tim made a deal with Mom to quit the team if his grades started suffering, don't you?" she asked in a sweet voice I knew was spiced with venom. "According to Tim, that was your idea, too."

"Look, Kathy," I pleaded, "I feel terrible. I really do. And I didn't mean to encourage Tim to chase after Marcy Cummings. Why would I want to do that? It's just that he kept talking about how great she was and this and that, and I was afraid he wouldn't like *me* anymore if I said I loathed someone he cared about, so I just—well, I just sort of agreed with him," I finished lamely.

"Annie, what's wrong with you?" Kathy sounded so confused and disappointed in me that the tears I'd been holding back all week started to fall.

"Oh, Kathy, I've just made a mess of my whole life! You were right," I told her. "I was a fool to start being a pal to all the guys, but I didn't know how else to act. If I change the way I act, they'll probably all hate me, including Tim!"

"Of course they won't hate you. You can change for the better, you know. Look, Annie, don't cry, please. I didn't know you were so unhappy. I didn't mean to yell at you, honest. It's just that I'm really upset about this Tim thing."

"I just want him to like me," I said, sobbing.

"Well, you don't have to be someone's doormat to get a boy to like you," she said calmly. "It's not honest, to you or anybody else. Why don't you just be yourself? Why don't you treat Tim and the rest of the boys more like you treat other girls?"

"W-what do you mean by that?" I stammered.

"Well, I mean if I were hung up on some boy who was as big a nerd as Marcy is and I kept babbling about how wonderful he was, you wouldn't keep telling me I was right, would you? You'd either not say anything at all, or you'd tell me you didn't like him. Don't you see, Annie? In some ways, you don't treat boys any better than Marcy does. That's terrible."

"But now all the guys count on me for advice," I wailed.

"So?" I could picture her shrugging her shoulders. "They'll get over it. They got along without your help before. And pretty soon, they'll stop thinking of you as a buddy and start seeing you as a real live girl instead."

"I guess you're right," I said slowly, then

sighed, feeling hopeless. "Even if I become an outcast, I guess it's better than being a one-girl information booth."

"*Or* an advice-to-the-lovelorn column," Kathy agreed. "And, Annie, will you please just shut up from now on when Tim brings up the subject of Marcy Cummings? That girl is screwing up his life."

"I—I won't encourage him to keep seeing her," I promised hesitantly, knowing how hard that was going to be. "I promise."

"Good!" Then in her brisk, no-nonsense way, Kathy changed the subject as abruptly as if we'd never been discussing it at all and started asking me all about my day.

Of course, deciding you're going to do something is always a whole lot easier than actually doing it. When I finally said goodbye to Kathy and hung up the phone, I joined Mom and Dad in the living room, where they were watching TV; but even though the show was one of my favorites, my mind couldn't concentrate on it. I was trying to imagine myself bluntly cutting Tim off the next time he started talking about Marcy. Just thinking about it made me feel sick to my stomach.

Maybe, I thought desperately, Tim will

just drop Marcy and never mention her name in front of me again. But I knew I was dreaming.

However, before I had to disappoint Tim, I got to practice my "no advice" motto on another boy. Doug Ruffner was the unlucky one. His locker was near mine, and one day he came over to where I was standing, getting my books, to tell me Sandy didn't think he should be allowed a night out with the boys.

"She says when a couple's going steady, they shouldn't need stuff like that anymore," he told me. "But I think she's wrong. Everybody needs more than one friend. How can I make Sandy understand?"

A whole lot of advice was on the tip of my tongue just waiting to come pouring out when I remembered my vow to myself. Taking a deep breath, I said evenly, "Since I've never gone steady, I don't think I'm the one to help you out, Doug."

He looked as surprised as if I'd suddenly confessed I was an undercover agent or something. "But you've told me what you thought about other things before, Annie!" he protested.

113

I nodded. "I know, Doug, but believe me, I think you were really the one who made things work out then. Anyway I'm not qualified to give advice." I gave him a smile that I hoped was sympathetic. "Don't worry, Doug. I'm sure you and Sandy will work it out."

He looked at me strangely, and at first, from the tight set of his lips, I could tell he was mad at me for not helping. Then he shrugged, and his expression mellowed. "Maybe you're right. I guess we should start working out things on our own and stop depending on other people."

"But I sure wish *somebody* could talk some sense into Sandy," he added, banging his hand not too violently against the row of lockers. "Sometimes she acts so hysterical and oversensitive, I could scream. I mean, look at you, Annie, you're not like that. You're calm and understanding. How come Sandy can't be?"

"It's easy for me to be calm, Doug," I said, the words ringing through the air before I'd really considered what I was about to say. "After all, I've got nothing to lose, have I? I'm not your girlfriend, and Sandy is, and that means she's got to see everything from a whole different perspective."

He slowly nodded his head. "You may have a point there." Then he grinned, and, opening his locker, started gathering up his books and jacket. "Maybe we just like to argue all the time so we can have the fun of making up. That's what Sandy's mom keeps telling us. Oh, here's Sandy now!"

I said goodbye to Doug and started down the hall, smiling hello at Sandy as I passed by, but to my surprise, she stopped, not in her usual hurry to get to Doug.

"What were you doing, Annie?" she asked, her voice sounding small and strange. "Giving Doug some more pointers on keeping me in line?"

I blushed to the roots of my hair, but I knew I deserved at least a little of Sandy's scorn. Maybe if our places had been reversed, I'd have felt the same way. "As a matter of fact, Sandy, I was explaining to Doug that I don't think there's any problem the two of you can't work out between yourselves." And I added, with every ounce of honesty in my whole body, "I'd give anything to have a steady relationship like the two of you do."

"Really?" The sour expression left her face, and she smiled. "Well, listen, don't worry, Annie, I'm sure you will one day." She straightened her shoulders and lifted her chin as she looked over to where Doug was waiting for her by the lockers. "I'd better run before *he* gets mad." She giggled, then started to walk away but turned back, saying seriously, "By the way, I really appreciate your telling him to keep our business between the two of us. I think we can work things out, too."

Doug and Sandy's reaction to the new, unhelpful me made me feel as if some kind of weight had been lifted off my shoulders. For one thing, Doug didn't seem to mind that I wouldn't tell him what to do. For another, Sandy actually seemed to like me better for not giving him my opinion.

Of course, I hadn't really expected the new me to upset the girls—after all, most of them had resented my friendliness to the guys in the first place. But if all the guys were as unconcerned as Doug, maybe I could keep my friendships with them even without continuing to serve as the local guidance counselor.

But as I walked home with a lighter step, I knew there was still a big bridge to be crossed, the biggest one of all. No matter how much I thought in terms of "all the guys," it wasn't all of them I was really worried about. If every boy except one in the sophomore class of Castle Heights High School worshiped the ground I walked on and if that one was Tim O'Hara and he couldn't stand me, then I knew I'd be a failure in my own eyes.

Chapter Ten

Without a doubt I was far from optimistic about Tim's reception of the new me. I'm not sure why I felt that. Maybe because I'd always gone so far out of the way to help him before; maybe I was sure he couldn't really like me for myself if he could like somebody as plastic as Marcy Cummings; or maybe it was just the bleak, wet January weather that had set in with a vengeance. Whatever reason, for the first time I could remember, I was making a big point of avoiding Tim, hoping against hope things would be all over between him and Marcy by the time we spoke again.

But by the second week of January, when

the New Year's Revue was playing Friday and Saturday nights, Tim and Marcy were still together. And with my luck, Carole and I just happened to choose Saturday night to go—the night Tim showed up with you-know-who by his side.

I watched the two of them walk down the aisle. Marcy was hanging all over Tim, and he was grinning down at her as if she were the most adorable thing he'd ever seen. Exactly what did Tim think was so wonderful about her? I just couldn't figure it out.

"You know what I really don't like about Marcy Cummings?" Carole asked, as if she could read my mind.

I stared at her in amazement and anticipation, shaking my head.

"I hate the way she does everything, even walking down an aisle here, as if she were in the movies or being photographed. You know what I mean? And it's as if no one else is really important to her except as something to hold on to. I always suspect that any one of her friends is exchangeable for another so far as Miss Marcy's concerned. Isn't there a word for that?"

"Egocentric?" I suggested. "I think that

means a person who always sees himself or herself as being at the center of everything."

"Yeah, that's her, all right," Carole said firmly, nodding her head. "Egocentric!"

The lights dimmed then, and the band started playing the overture for this year's revue, a series of songs, skits, and dances put on by kids from all grades and written by the senior class. In the fading brightness of the auditorium, I could see Marcy's fair hair swaying gently toward Tim's head of dark, tousled curls as she leaned to whisper something in his ear, and I thought about what Carole had said.

It was true, I decided. Marcy didn't seem really to care much about anyone. Every time I'd ever seen her with Tim, she seemed more interested in who was watching them than in Tim himself. It was as if she saw herself as part of a picture, with a tall, handsome, dark-haired boy setting off her dainty, blond beauty. I wondered if she'd ever seen Tim as a person or thought about what he was like inside.

That thought made me sadder than anything. Sure, Tim was adorable, and I knew he was one of the more popular boys in the sophomore class, but what I really liked about

120

him was the way he joked and talked and the easy way he had of walking next to me, never making me feel pressured to be cute or witty. When I thought about Marcy being too caught up in herself to notice any of that in Tim, it made me feel almost sorry for her.

The second the lights went up after the revue, I grabbed Carole's arm. "Let's leave for Pop's now so we can get a good table," I said, hustling down the aisle.

"I think we can be the first ones there without doing the fifty-yard dash, Annie!" She was laughing, but there was an edge to her voice that made me slow down.

"OK," I said, giving a little shrug.

It was dark outside, and the streetlights were casting such heavy shadows I couldn't see Carole's face clearly when she said, "Anyhow, Annie, I know the real reason you were hurrying away from the crowd."

I was glad she couldn't see mine when I answered, "What do you mean? What's so odd about wanting to get a good booth at Pop's?"

"Nothing. But just about everyone in school knows you're crazy about Tim O'Hara, Annie, so you may as well admit it." Sounding a little hurt, she added, "And I don't think

121

there's any reason to keep something like that from your friends—if you trust them."

She was right, I thought. "I didn't think anybody knew," I said weakly.

"Annie Wainwright!" she scolded. "All anybody's got to do to get the picture is look at you for two seconds when you're staring at Tim as if he were a hot fudge sundae you were about to devour!"

"Oh, no!" I groaned. "Is it that obvious?"

"Well, not really," she admitted. "But I spotted it awhile ago, so why are you pretending your big hurry *isn't* because you don't want to run into him with Marcy?"

"Because I feel like such a fool!" I blurted out, relieved at being able to tell someone how I really felt. "Tim hardly even knows I'm alive except when he needs advice, and I just can't bear to see him with that awful girl! Oh, Carole, I'm so confused!"

"So is this the way you're solving things? By running away from the two of them and acting as if you've done something wrong?"

"I can't keep pretending to Tim that I like her and think it's terrific he's dating her!" I moaned.

"Who says you've got to?" We were getting closer to Pop's now, and I slowed down, walking more slowly even though it was bone-chillingly cold outside and I could hardly wait for the steam heat to envelop me. I wanted to finish this conversation before we got to the pizza parlor.

"I know, I know. But I just don't know how to act anymore, Carole."

"Why don't you just act the way you always have? I mean, I know it sounds trite, but why don't you try just being yourself?" she asked. "If you don't want Tim to burden you with his troubles, don't let him. You can be unselfish without being an absolute *martyr*, for goodness' sake! And how in the world do you expect Tim to know you're interested if you continue to give him advice about Marcy? It doesn't make sense to me."

We got to the door then, and I quickly started talking about the revue. Carole caught my eye, then went along with it, and I guess it wasn't hard for her to understand that, in the middle of a restaurant, I didn't want to discuss anything as painful as Tim's relationship with Marcy.

Since we'd rushed over there, we were just about through by the time the place really started filling up, and we were at the register paying our check when Marcy sailed in the door with Tim shyly trailing behind her.

"Don't tell me you guys are leaving already?" Tim asked, looking disappointed.

Before Carole or I could do anything but nod, Marcy was pouting and tugging on his arm. "C'mon, Tim, let's sit down before all the good booths are taken!"

"I swear I'd rather become a hermit than have to act like that to get a guy!" I vowed fervently as we walked along the icy road toward my house.

"You're getting as dramatic as Kathy!" Carole laughed, not taking me seriously at all.

"I don't see what's so funny!"

"There's a huge difference between being all alone and not having a boyfriend. I mean, do you feel sorry for me because *I* don't have a boyfriend?"

Carole sounded so matter-of-fact and concerned that I stared at her in amazement before I realized with a jolt that I'd never considered the fact that Carole didn't date much. And now that I did, nothing seemed wrong with it. "But, Carole, you're different," I insisted. "You're tall and pretty and sure of yourself. If boys don't ask you out, it doesn't mean something is wrong with *you*."

"Then why does it mean something is wrong with *you*?" she countered.

I stopped, trying to think of how to explain it so Carole would understand. Then I saw that she was right. I'd made up my mind something was hideously wrong with me that made me repel all the boys. It was like a self-fulfilling prophecy. I didn't give them a chance to like me as a girl, so they didn't, and then I was even *more* convinced I was not likable, and so forth.

"All right, all right," I said, giving in laughingly, feeling a lot better already. "So I'm not a leper. What do you suggest, doctor?" I asked, smiling to think how often I was asking other people for advice lately.

"I'm no expert, but I'd say forget about it for a while. If somebody asks you out, fine. If they don't, fine. There's more to life than boys, Annie."

"Yes, but—"

"And even if there isn't," she interrupted tartly, "moping about it certainly won't change anything."

"You're right," I said wholeheartedly. "Boy, have I been wasting a lot of time lately. C'mon, let's go get some of Mom's cookies before Dad takes you home. Suddenly I'm starved again!" We ran up the front path to my house.

As the days passed, I was more and more grateful to have friends like Kathy and Carole—friends who cared enough to tell me how they really felt. I knew Kathy had been right about the "support" I gave Tim. If I'd really wanted to be his friend, I should have been as blunt with him as my friends had been with me.

I got my chance to practice what I was, well, not exactly *preaching*—since I wasn't doing any more of that these days—but to practice what I was *thinking* less than a week after the New Year's Revue. Tim was standing by the front door when school ended, and he gave me a smile when he saw me heading down the hall. Uh-oh, I thought, this is it! And I was right.

"Heading home, Annie?" he asked.

I just nodded, and sure enough, his next words were, "Mind if I walk with you?"

"Of course not, Tim. I like to walk with you," I told him sincerely, not adding that I liked it until he brought up Marcy. But today was different, anyway. As we talked about this and that, casually bouncing from subject to subject, I was actually looking forward to the moment he'd start heaping his problems on my shoulders.

Finally, it came. "Can you believe Marcy's going to the February Formal with Barry?" Tim asked in disbelief.

"I asked her how early she expected me to ask her, and she just said she was sorry but Barry got there first." He groaned. "You've got to help me, Annie! How can I convince her to break her date with him?"

Here goes, I said to myself, sure I'd be driving Tim away forever. But I'd made up my mind, and I was determined to go through with it. "Frankly, Tim, I don't know why you bother," I said, watching the stunned look come over his face at my words. "I mean, Marcy doesn't seem to care about going to the dance with you. If you were dating *me*, *I* wouldn't accept a date with Barry at all."

"But—but you know Marcy thinks she should date more than one guy because of her shyness!" he protested, rising to her defense. "How can you blame her?"

We'd reached the O'Haras' house and stopped. Hugging my books to my chest, I looked him straight in the eye and, hardly able to breathe, told him, "Look, Tim, to tell

127

you the truth, I'd rather not discuss Marcy anymore. I don't think she's good enough for you, and I don't especially like her. As far as I'm concerned, whatever goes on between the two of you is none of my business. If you have problems with Marcy, talk to *her* about them."

Tim was looking at me as if seeing me for the first time, and he didn't appear to like what he saw. His forehead creased, and his eyes narrowed as if he were trying to figure out some deeper meaning to what I had said. "I thought you were my friend, Annie," he accused me.

"I am, Tim. Really I am. And that's exactly why I'm telling you this. I realized I haven't been a very good friend lately. If I were, I would have been honest instead of encouraging you to keep seeing a girl who I think doesn't deserve you."

He shook his head slowly, still staring at me in amazement. "Thanks for the help," he finally muttered sarcastically, stomping away through the light dusting of snow.

"Tim, I'm sorry!" I called after him, but he didn't turn, and I continued home on legs that had turned to lead. All right, I'd done the right thing. My conscience was clear.

Now—would Tim and I ever straighten things out?

I didn't change my decision, though, even though the next few days were rough. No matter what boy approached me, I didn't let myself get roped into solving his problems. I just tried to boost his spirits the way I would do with my girlfriends.

And I forced myself to *make* conversation. I'd change the subject as offhandedly as I could, talking about normal, everyday things like movies or school. I refused to behave as if guys wouldn't want to talk to me unless they were getting helpful hints in return. And you know what? It worked!

For the first time since sophomore year started, I was really enjoying myself. And Carole and Kathy were right in more ways than one, I understood. For example, I was learning that not having dates wasn't the end of the world. I could have fun doing other things—with guys *and* girls.

One day as I was standing at my locker after the last period, Kathy came up to me. "Want to go to Pop's?" she asked. "Kurt and I are going, and I just ran into Carole, who said she was starved and would meet us there in awhile."

"Well, sure," I said, hesitating for just a second.

"Don't worry," Kathy said reassuringly. "Tim and Marcy won't be there."

So I went, walking along easily with Kathy and Kurt and not feeling at all out of place.

When we arrived at Pop's, we were greeted by Barry and Kenny, who called us over to their table. We all sat in a big, noisy bunch, and Carole joined us later.

I had a great time, laughing and eating. But the best part was the talking. I talked to Barry about our last geometry test, which had been very unfair, and to Kenny about the sad state of TV sitcoms, and to Kurt about Kathy's part in the New Year's Revue. Not once did anyone bring up a problem. Suddenly I thought, *This is great, Annie, and you're making it happen. You can be part of a crowd. You just have to work at it.*

After we finished off a pizza, we all had to split up, and Kathy and I ended up walking home alone together. She talked about the February Formal and the new dress she'd bought, then stopped and asked carefully, "You're still not going to the formal, Annie?"

"I guess not." I sighed. "And it's not like I'm sitting around waiting for Tim, and Tim alone, to ask me. I'd go with someone else. But, you know what? I don't care so much. I'm having too much fun doing things like going to Pop's with everyone. But," I added, "I sure do wish I were going with Tim."

Kathy put her arm around me. "I'm sure you'll work it out," she said. "You seem to be working everything else out. You know what I'll do, though?"

"What? You're not giving me any advice, are you?"

"Absolutely not." She laughed. "I'll just let it be known around our house that you don't have a date. Maybe that will set Tim thinking."

I nodded. "It can't hurt. Thanks a lot, Kathy." By the time I reached home, I felt very happy.

The only real black cloud that marred my new good feelings was Tim's attitude. Oh, he waved to me when we passed in the corridors and said hi and stuff like that, but he sure wasn't seeking me out. And from the drawn, sullen look on his face as he stalked through the halls, I could tell he was going through some unpleasant changes.

I asked Kathy about him one night when

she stayed to dinner at our house. We were lingering over coffee at the kitchen table.

"How's—how's Tim been lately?" I asked hesitantly.

"You mean, did I manage to drop the hint about the dance?"

"Well, no, not that so much as—oh, I don't know. He seems so distant lately."

"Yeah. He's been sort of withdrawn. I can't tell what's going on in his mind. I see Marcy and him together, but he couldn't be very happy."

"Do you think he's mad at me?" I asked.

Kathy gazed out the window. "I don't know. I really don't know. He's so close-mouthed these days. Look, Annie, you're my best friend, and Tim's my twin, and I love you both—but I will not get caught between you. I don't want to be a go-between."

"I understand," I said softly.

"I'm not going to desert you, though," she went on. "So I will give you some advice."

"Are you sure you should?" I asked.

"Just this once," she said, smiling. "I think for now you should do nothing, except go on being as pleasant to Tim as always. He's the one who's being unreasonable and has got to come to his senses."

"All right," I said, feeling resigned.

But it wasn't easy.

I still saw him with Marcy, so I figured he was sticking with her no matter what anyone said. I didn't think they were getting along any better, though, especially after I saw her walk away from him one day and say angrily, "If there's one thing I just hate, it's a boy who acts like he owns me!"

I ducked into a doorway until Tim had turned and stalked away. I could tell he was furious, and I didn't want to make things worse by letting him know I'd witnessed that unpleasant little scene.

But to be perfectly honest, I was too busy to worry much about Tim. I knew he was still the boy I adored, but if he didn't want me, there wasn't much I could do about it. In the meantime, I was doing what I could about myself. I was working harder than ever for the paper, and I'd started having kids over to the house every now and then.

Since we lived near the school, it was only natural for my friends to start hanging out at my place once I opened my mouth and invited them. Sometimes in the afternoon, a bunch of sophomores would drop by, or at night, Kurt and Kathy or Kenny and Barry would stop in, bringing albums to play or homework to do.

I even had a date! It was with Kenny, and we just went to the movies. Disappointingly, it was no big deal. Or maybe that wasn't so disappointing, after all. The whole experience showed me how much I'd overemphasized the importance of dating. I mean, I liked Kenny and all, and we had a nice time, but after it was all over, I didn't feel the slightest bit different—about him or myself—in spite of the fact that he'd put his arm around me during the movie and kissed me, then kissed me again when we were parked in his car after he'd brought me home.

So I guess you could say I was adjusting to the life of an average high-school sophomore. Nothing was spectacular. Everything was sort of normal. And then, just as I was feeling pretty good, Tim O'Hara came along and shook everything up.

Chapter Eleven

One day between classes I frantically rushed to my locker. As I reached inside to grab a book, I became aware of someone leaning against the wall next to me, and out of the corner of my eye, I caught sight of kelly-green wool and knew it was Tim's sweater.

"Hi, Tim," I said a little unsteadily as I looked up.

He smiled his old crooked smile, the one that crinkled his eyes and showed his perfect teeth.

"Hi, Annie," he said in a voice so low and husky a little shiver went through me. I hadn't expected his nearness to have the same effect on me it had before, and I was a little shaken to realize nothing had changed.

"What's up?" I asked, my voice unnaturally high as I tried to sound supercasual.

His eyes left mine, and he shuffled his books around as if he didn't know what to do next. Finally, he mumbled, "I—I just wanted to apologize for the way I acted the other week." He raised his green eyes then, and my heart skipped a beat as they met mine. "I was behaving like a real moron, and I know it." He sounded almost angry again.

"Oh, it's all right," I said, not knowing what else I *could* say. "I guess I must have surprised you."

"Yeah. Well, it was more than that. You said everything to me I'd been thinking about and trying not to admit. That's why I jumped at you."

"You mean about—?"

He nodded so abruptly his dark curls shook. "About Marcy. Yeah, I guess I knew all the time she was just leading me on. I'm a sucker for a challenge, I suppose," he admitted, smiling a little at last. "Anyhow, I wondered if you—if you'd like to go to the February Formal with me. If you don't have a date already, that is."

Talk about being surprised! After everything that had happened, Tim O'Hara was finally asking me to the February Formal! But I was very cool as I answered, "Oh, Tim, that would be terrific."

The bell rang then, so he just said, "Great!" and gave me a quick grin before dashing off.

My heart pounded as I raced to English class, and if I hadn't known better, I'd have been scared it was going to pop right out of my chest. But within ten minutes, all my excitement had disappeared.

Tim had probably just said all that stuff about Marcy for my sake, I told myself miserably. He'd probably take her to the dance in an instant if she'd break her date with Barry. And since he was undoubtedly still under Marcy's spell, who better to ask to the formal than Annie Wainwright, a real pal as opposed to a real *girl*, someone safe in Tim's eyes, someone he'd never dream of getting involved with?

Ordinarily I'd have let doubts like these drift by, ignoring them or rationalizing them away, but now that I was used to talking more and being more open and honest with people, I decided at least to broach the subject to Tim. I finally got up the nerve when I ran into him one afternoon on my walk home from school.

"Tim," I said, finally, my heart pounding, "I'm so happy you invited me to the February Formal, but there's something I have to ask you."

"What?"

"Well, if Marcy weren't going with Barry, wouldn't you rather take her?"

For a couple of seconds, Tim looked like he might explode, but then he seemed to calm down and said, "I guess that's a fair question. And the answer is no, I would not rather take Marcy. That's all over."

I must still have been looking a little uncertain because Tim moved closer to me and hesitantly put his arm around my shoulders. Then he looked deep into my eyes and said, "Annie, I think you're a really great girl. The best."

I wanted to melt away right there, feeling Tim's arm around me and looking into his sparkling, serious eyes, but instead I just smiled at him, and Tim smiled back, making my heart pound even faster.

After a scene like that, you'd think I could

forget all about Marcy Cummings. But I couldn't. I mean, hadn't Tim told me before that I was great and the best? It hadn't meant anything then; why should it mean something now?

But then I forced myself to stop trying to analyze *why* Tim was taking me to the dance, and I decided just to go and have fun with him. If nothing ever came of the whole thing but this one date, at least I'd have that. I pushed my fears to the background and did everything but swear on a stack of Bibles to have the best time of my life at the dance.

Needless to say, Mom was thrilled that her daughter had turned into Cinderella at last. She even gave me an extra twenty dollars to add to the money I took out of my savings for a dress. And I found the most beautiful dress in the whole world, a silky wisp of dark blue roses on a lighter blue background, with spaghetti straps and a nipped-in waist that showed off my slim new figure. With my olive skin and dark hair, I looked as exotic as a South Seas beauty.

Tim borrowed his dad's car for the occasion and came to pick me up. When he arrived, we walked arm in arm into the living room to say goodbye to Mom and Dad. In his dark suit and pale blue shirt, Tim looked as if he'd walked straight off the cover of a magazine, and as I caught a glimpse of us in the hall mirror, even I had to admit we made a terrific-looking couple.

Of course, Mom and Dad had to get out the camera and take pictures, but that was OK because Tim kept his arm draped securely across my shoulders the whole time, and we kept looking into each other's eyes and laughing. When Dad left the room to put the camera away and Mom went to find my coat, Tim turned to face me. He put both hands on my bare shoulders, and I wished I could stand that way forever, feeling the touch of his hands. "Annie," he said, looking both serious and a little scared, "you're beautiful. I've wanted to tell you that for a long time." Then he kissed his hand and touched his fingers to my cheek.

As we drove to school, I wondered how Marcy would react when she saw me with Tim. No one except Kathy knew I was his date. And Kathy, of course, thought it was just wonderful.

We reached the school and parked in the

jammed lot. Tim escorted me in. I was carrying the gardenia he'd given me in its box, along with the silver evening bag I'd borrowed from Mom. I didn't want to pin on the corsage until I'd hung up my coat and gone to the girls' room to fix my lipstick. The last thing I wanted was my first corsage to turn brown before the evening even got under way!

Tim waited for me in the hall, and my heart swelled with pleasure at the way his face lit up when he spotted me. I knew he was happy to be with me.

The gym was transformed. "Oh, it's beautiful, isn't it?" I whispered as we stood in the center of the room, looking up at the yards and yards of white crepe paper and cotton that had been skillfully arranged to turn the room into a winter wonderland.

"Mmm," Tim agreed, grinning, "but not as pretty as you."

The dance band started playing a slow song, and Tim put his hand lightly on my back. "Want to dance?"

All I could do was nod as he took me into his arms. I'd been dreaming of this moment for so long, and now that it was finally here, I was afraid I'd be too dazed to be able to remember it.

141

But I do. I remember almost every single second of that night. I remember watching Kurt sweep by with Kathy held lightly in his arms as if she were a fragile doll. I remember Carole Deutsch's eyes shining as she gazed up at Billy Dempsey, her first important date. I remember the lilt of the music and the taste of the punch and a sort of whirl of lights and decorations and faces. And I'll never forget the wonderful soapy smell of Tim's cheek as he held me close or the feel of his jacket where my hand rested on his shoulder.

And I'll never forget Marcy Cummings.

She almost wrecked the entire night for me.

I excused myself about two hours after we'd gotten there to run back to the girls' room to freshen up, and who should be there primping in front of the mirror but Marcy. I smiled as blandly as I could and, after searching through my bag, began to comb my hair. From time to time I could feel her eyes on me in the mirror, and I wondered if she suspected that in between I was studying her just as closely. She looked pretty, I had to admit, in a slinky dress of lavender knit that made her skin look white as milk.

Then suddenly her eyes caught mine. Embarrassed, I blurted out, "That's a beautiful dress, Marcy."

"Oh, this? Thank you, Annie. Yours is . . . cute, too." She said it sweetly enough but managed to imply something was horribly wrong with it.

I hurriedly put on my lipstick, trying to get out of there as fast as I could. But I was too late. Snapping her bag closed, Marcy turned from the sink and faced me. "I just wanted to thank you for babysitting Tim for me, Annie," she said in a little-girl voice.

"What?" I gulped.

"You know, for making sure Tim had a date." She laughed lightly. "I did explain to him that it was too late for me to break off with Barry but that I didn't mind if he went with someone else." She paused, then added, "As long as it wasn't a *real* date, of course."

It was several minutes before I felt collected enough to leave the girls' room. Of course, I thought, I'd been right all along. Tim had only asked me because I wasn't a threat to him or to Marcy. He'd never really broken up with her.

For a while I was tempted to sneak away

and leave. But thankfully, I calmed down. When I was myself again, I saw that I'd be a fool to let Marcy's words ruin the nicest night of my life. What if Tim *were* still hung up on her? He was certainly being attentive—more than attentive, at times. Maybe he would have preferred a coy, experienced fox like her, but he was with me, and we were having fun, and there wasn't any reason not to keep on having fun no matter what might happen tomorrow.

With that resolution in my mind, I rejoined Tim at the refreshment table. And it didn't take long for me to put Marcy totally out of my thoughts.

She only reentered them hours later. We'd gone to Pop's with Kurt and Kathy, laughing and talking, doing whatever we could not to let the evening end. All too soon, we were looking at our watches and groaning about our curfews. And then Tim and I were sitting in his father's car, pulled up at the curb in front of my house.

He pulled me toward him gently and let his lips just lightly brush mine. "I had a wonderful time, Annie," he said softly. "Really great."

Maybe because his kiss had brought so many different emotions rushing to the surface, I spoke before I could think. "Better than you'd have had with Marcy?" I pulled myself away.

"Hey!" His voice cracked. "What's the big idea? Why are you dragging Marcy into this?"

"She told me in the bathroom that she'd given you permission to go with someone like me," I said stiffly. "I understand I'm not a *real* date for you, Tim, so you don't have to humor me." Then, embarrassed by my outburst, I added, "But I really did have a good time, the best time ever. Thanks for asking me."

I started to slide out the door, but Tim grabbed my hand and pulled me back. "Just a second! You're talking nonsense, and I think I've got a right to know why. Do you mean Marcy filled your head with all this garbage? And you believed her?"

"Look, Tim," I said, sorry I'd started the whole thing, "it's all right. Honest, it is. I know how you feel about Marcy. And I know how you feel about me."

He shook his head vigorously. "No, you don't. Or you wouldn't be talking this way."

145

That shut me up, and he went on. "Look, Annie, I did fall for Marcy. But I admit I made a mistake. I see her now for what she is. I don't hate her. Actually, I feel a little sorry for her for having to use guys the way she does, and I'm ashamed of myself for allowing her to use *me*. But I'm not hung up on her anymore, and I certainly didn't have to get her *permission* to go to the formal with you or anyone else."

"You mean she said that just to upset me?"

"That's what it sounds like. She probably didn't think you'd dare mention it to me and get set straight."

"But why would Marcy go out of her way like that to hurt me?"

He laughed lightly, and his arm was suddenly around my shoulder again. "Maybe because I made the mistake of confessing to her once that before I started dating her, you were the girl I'd been trying to get up the nerve to ask out."

"Me?" My voice was a high squeak. "You were trying to get up the nerve to ask *me* out? But, Tim," I protested, "you kept asking for advice about Marcy."

"Yeah, I started that because I figured I could tell by your reaction whether or not you were interested. And when you didn't try to discourage me from asking her out, I figured you didn't find me as irresistible as I'd been hoping! So then I *did* ask Marcy out, and she was so sweet and pretty and flattering I got trapped by her."

I remembered that afternoon in Pop's when I'd thought he was hinting around to ask me out and instead asked about Marcy. I let out a loud groan. "Oh, Tim, why didn't you just ask me?"

"I don't know. It was dumb. But you seemed to know how to deal with everything, Annie. I guess I was intimidated."

"Oh, boy!" I laughed. "Some team we are!"

He laughed, too. Then all of a sudden, he wasn't laughing anymore, and the hand on my shoulder was gently pulling me closer. "Yeah, some team," he whispered as his lips gently came down on mine for a real kiss this time, a real kiss for a real girl.

It's June now, almost the end of my sophomore year. And what a year this has been. I've sure learned a lot. For starters, I'm not the scared lump I was nine months ago. Now I know I can win or lose friends on the basis of myself alone and not because of what I can do for them or how I can help them out. After all, how good was I as "Dear Annie" in the long run?

One bright day that felt more like the beginning of summer than the end of spring, Tim met me at lunchtime. "Want to take a picnic to Bear Creek Park?" he asked.

It was exam week, and neither of us had afternoon exams.

"Sure!" I said, happy to escape the pressure of studying—and to be able to spend some time alone with him.

"Great. We can pick up sandwiches at Pop's."

An hour later we pulled into the Bear Creek parking lot, and I grabbed the bag from Pop's, and Tim took the old blue blanket from the back seat of the car. We held hands and ran breathlessly down a grassy hillside to the creek below. Then we walked along the bank until we found a shady place by some boulders that looked private and quiet.

We spread out the blanket and sat down on it.

"Want to eat now?" asked Tim.

"No," I said, smiling, and reached for his hand.

Tim flashed me his lopsided grin and lay down on the blanket.

"I'm exhausted," he said. "Thank goodness I've got only two more exams."

"Yeah," I agreed. I laced my fingers through his and ran my other hand through his dark curls.

"Just think," Tim murmured, "this summer we can swim together, bike together, picnic together—all we want. I'm going to be home all summer."

"Me, too," I said, smiling a secret smile as I remembered last summer when Tim had gone off to Canada and later I had read up on Banff just so I could make conversation with him.

"Annie," Tim said suddenly, sitting up and taking both my hands in his, "I—I want to ask you something, and you don't have to answer now if you don't want to. You can wait until you're ready."

"What?" I asked, looking intently into his eyes.

"Annie, will you go steady with me?"

I could feel my hands tremble a little in his, and he held them tighter.

"Yes," I said. "I don't think we need to wait any longer to be sure it's right."

"Is that your advice?" he asked, his eyes sparkling.

"Yes." I laughed. "The last I'll ever give."

Then Tim wrapped me in his strong arms and placed his lips on mine in a tender kiss.

It was love at first sight . . .

NEVER LOVE A COWBOY
Jesse DuKore

Bitsy is thrilled when she moves from crowded New York City to colorful Austin, Texas, and even more thrilled when she sees handsome Billy Joe riding his horse to school. For Bitsy, it's love at first sight.

But even when Bitsy's new school radio program grabs everyone's attention, Billy Joe's eye remains on gorgeous Betty Lou. Can a city girl like Bitsy ever win the heart of a Texas cowboy like Billy Joe?

Nina would do almost anything for Scott. . . .

LITTLE WHITE LIES
Lois I. Fisher

Everyone says Nina has a good imagination, a gift for telling stories. In fact, it's one of her stories that attracts Scott to her. He's one of the Daltonites, the most sophisticated clique in the school. Nina can't believe she's dating him!

But Nina soon finds that the Daltonites don't welcome outsiders. So she impresses Scott's friends with her stories. It's so easy; a little exaggeration here, a little white lie there.

I'm doing this for Scott, she thinks. But her lies finally start to catch up with her, and Nina's afraid of losing Scott forever.

Is Killy too young for love?

TOO YOUNG FOR LOVE
Gailanne Maravel

It looks like Tom and Killy's friendship is turning into romance . . . but then Tom finds out she's two years younger than the other kids in school.

Killy is miserable, until she leaves the whole mess behind, for a glamorous vacation in Italy.

When she gets back, she feels sophisticated and grown up. But will Tom think so, too?

She had two special loves . . . .

TRUSTING HEARTS
Jocelyn Saal

When Kathy lands an after-school job as the assistant to the town's veterinarian, she knows she's found a career she'll always love. At the same time, her old friend Dean has become more tender and romantic toward her.

Kathy's overjoyed, until Dean starts resenting the long hours she puts in at the animal hospital, and their new love seems about to fall apart. She'd be lost without Dean, but she loves her new job just as much. Will she have to make a choice between them?

SWEET DREAMS

We hope you enjoyed reading this book. All the titles currently available in the Sweet Dreams series are listed on the next page. Ask for them in your local bookshop or newsagent. Two new titles are published each month.

If you would like to know more about Sweet Dreams, or if you have difficulty obtaining any of the books locally, or if you would like to tell us what you think of the series, write to:—

Kim Prior,
Corgi Books,
Century House,
61-63 Uxbridge Road,
London W5 5SA

☐	20323 1	P.S. I LOVE YOU	Barbara Conklin	65p
☐	20325 8	POPULARITY PLAN	Rosemary Vernon	65p
☐	20327 4	LAURIE'S SONG	Suzanne Rand	65p
☐	20328 2	PRINCESS AMY	Melinda Pollowitz	65p
☐	20326 6	LITTLE SISTER	Yvonne Greene	65p
☐	20324 X	CALIFORNIA GIRL	Janet Quin-Harkin	65p
☐	20604 4	GREEN EYES	Suzanne Rand	65p
☐	20601 X	THE THOROUGHBRED	Joanne Campbell	65p
☐	20744 X	COVER GIRL	Yvonne Greene	65p
☐	20745 8	LOVE MATCH	Janet Quin-Harkin	65p
☐	20787 3	THE PROBLEM WITH LOVE		
			Rosemary Vernon	65p
☐	20788 1	NIGHT OF THE PROM		
			Debra Spector	65p
☐	17779 6	THE SUMMER JENNY FELL IN		
		LOVE	Barbara Conklin	75p
☐	17780 X	DANCE OF LOVE	Jocelyn Saal	75p
☐	17781 8	THINKING OF YOU	Jeannette Nobile	75p
☐	17782 6	HOW DO YOU SAY GOODBYE?		
			Margret Burman	75p
☐	17783 4	ASK ANNIE	Suzanne Rand	75p
☐	17784 2	TEN BOY SUMMER	Janet Quin-Harkin	75p
☐	22542 1	LOVE SONG	Anne Park	75p
☐	22682 7	THE POPULARITY SUMMER		
			Rosemary Vernon	75p
☐	22607 X	ALL'S FAIR IN LOVE	Jeanne Andrews	75p
☐	22683 5	SECRET IDENTITY	Joanne Campbell	75p
☐	17797 4	FALLING IN LOVE AGAIN	Barbara Conklin	75p
☐	17800 8	THE TROUBLE WITH CHARLIE		
			Joan Lowery Nixon	75p
☐	17795 8	HER SECRET SELF	Rhondi Villot	75p
☐	17796 6	IT MUST BE MAGIC	Marian Woodruff	75p
☐	17798 2	TOO YOUNG FOR LOVE	Gailanne Maravel	75p
☐	17801 6	TRUSTING HEARTS	Jocelyn Saal	75p
☐	17813 X	NEVER LOVE A COWBOY	Jesse Dukore	75p
☐	17814 8	LITTLE WHITE LIES	Lois I. Fisher	75p
☐	17839 3	TOO CLOSE FOR COMFORT	Debra Spector	75p
☐	17840 7	DAYDREAMER	Janet Quin-Harkin	75p
☐	17841 5	DEAR AMANDA	Rosemary Vernon	75p
☐	17842 3	COUNTRY GIRL	Melinda Pollowitz	75p
☐	17843 1	FORBIDDEN LOVE	Marian Woodruff	75p
☐	17844 X	SUMMER DREAMS	Barbara Conklin	75p
☐	17846 6	PORTRAIT OF LOVE	Jeannette Nobile	75p
☐	17847 4	RUNNING MATES	Jocelyn Saal	75p
☐	17848 2	FIRST LOVE	Debra Spector	75p
☐	17849 0	SECRETS	Anna Aaron	75p